Y0-AVB-129

A Toast to Cousin Julian

Also by Estelle Thompson

TO CATCH A RAINBOW
HUNTER IN THE DARK
FIND A CROOKED SIXPENCE

A TOAST TO COUSIN JULIAN

Estelle Thompson

Walker and Company
New York

Copyright © 1986, 1987 by Estelle Thompson

All rights reserved. No part of this book may be
reproduced or transmitted in any form or by any
means, electronic or mechanical, including photocopying,
recording or by any information storage and retrieval
system, without permission in writing from the Publisher.

All the characters and events portrayed in this story
are fictitious.

First published in the United States of America
in 1987 by the Walker Publishing Company, Inc.

Library of Congress Cataloging-in-Publication Data

Thompson, Estelle.
   A toast to Cousin Julian.

   I. Title.
PR9619.3.T447T63   1987   823   86-18894
ISBN 0-8027-5665-4

Printed in the United States of America

10 9 8 7 6 5 4 3 2 1

One

It was still raining steadily as I parked the car and ran up the stairs to the door of my flat, my mood as dreary and bleak as the weather.

The flare of anger in which I had quit my secretarial job had subsided, and though I still had no qualms about what I had done, the practical problems were beginning to surface. Jobs were not easy to get, especially for people without references, and after one or two things I'd said that day, my ex-employer was unlikely to be forthcoming with any glowing testimonials.

Rochelle, the up-and-coming model with whom I shared the flat, was already home, lying back in the best easy-chair with the totally relaxed grace of something feline. She looked up from a magazine and waved a coffee mug vaguely.

'There's coffee if you want it. You look a bit damp.' She looked at me more closely. 'In fact, you look a bit dampened. Spirits and all.'

'I suppose I am. I just quit my job.'

'Yoiks! I thought you were practically one of the office fixtures. What happened? Don't tell me poor old what's-his-name made a pass at you!'

I poured myself some coffee. 'Old what's-his-name is much too righteous to do any such thing. He only sacks cleaning-ladies who have about as much chance of getting another job as I have of being chosen Miss Universe.'

Rochelle raised a languid eyebrow. 'These things happen.

I suppose she just wasn't up to scratch. You have to be, Patricia my love. Up to scratch, I mean. Whatever your job. It's a jungle out there, as they say.'

'I'm aware of it,' I said. 'And she was up to scratch. That's the whole point. He claimed she'd taken some money out of his desk – oh, fifty dollars or something – said she was the only one who could have taken it. He called her in and sacked her on the spot. I hit the roof, I guess, because if the damned money was missing she certainly wasn't the only one who could have taken it – nor, in my opinion, was she by any means the most likely. But he'd made up his mind and wouldn't have any kind of investigation – didn't even tell her why she was dismissed, didn't ask anyone else any questions. When I protested with a certain amount of vigour, he told me it was none of my affair.'

Rochelle shrugged. 'He had a point, I guess.'

'I might have almost conceded that. But he said, "My dear Miss Kent, don't upset yourself. It's only the cleaning woman." That rather did it, I guess. I asked him if women who cleaned offices for a living had some magic formula whereby they didn't need homes or three meals a day. And I cleaned out my desk and left.'

'Well, well. Patricia for the people. Oh, and there's a letter for you on the table. It's from that furniture company your aunt or somebody left you shares in, according to the envelope. So cheer up, it's probably a handsome dividend cheque.'

'I'll probably need it,' I said dryly, picking up the envelope. 'Though the solicitor seemed to think the company wasn't exactly thriving.'

'Funny thing,' Rochelle said musingly, 'it hadn't registered – before, I mean, when you told me about inheriting shares in the company – I suppose I wasn't paying much attention. But when I saw the name on the envelope – Selbridge – it rang a bell. Something from away back. I've been sitting here trying to remember.'

I was the one not paying much attention now, though

part of my brain heard her.

'Some kind of scandal. No, it must have been more than that: a crime of some kind. And I mean, the company's away up in Queensland, so for the story to even make the Melbourne papers, let alone stick in my mind, it must have been something pretty big. Or unusual. Mustn't it?' she added insistently.

'You probably imagined it,' I said.

She shook her head. 'I'm sure I didn't. It must've made quite an impression on me at the time – so far away. Oh, and speaking of far-away places, Trish, guess what? I'm off to Perth for a year's contract with a modelling group. Isn't it exciting?'

I was frowning at the letter. 'Mmm,' I said.

'You haven't heard a word I've said!' Rochelle accused. 'Just how big *is* that dividend cheque?'

I put the letter down and sipped my coffee. 'It isn't,' I said. 'A cheque, I mean. It's an advice of an offer from a bigger company to buy Selbridges out. It's quite an attractive offer for a company that's rather been in the doldrums. They're having a formal meeting of the shareholders – if that's the proper term – partners is better, I suppose: there are only five of us. There has to be a decision on whether or not to sell. They've enclosed a form to enable me to cast a postal vote.'

'But that's splendid! If the company's flat you're never going to get anything out of it. If it's sold and you collect your share it'll more than help you over till you get another job, I presume?'

'Well and truly.'

'Then you'd better tick the square marked "sell", or whatever you have to do, and get the form back by return mail.'

I picked the letter up again and looked at it, not seeing it. Seeing instead a thin, grey-haired lady who had once been tall and strong and, to judge from an old photograph she'd once shown me, rather beautiful, with sparkling dark eyes and an impish tilt to her mouth when she smiled. When I knew her the tall form was slightly stooped and the beauty had faded, but not the sparkle in the eyes nor the imp in her smile.

'Well?' Rochelle sounded slightly impatient and I felt she'd probably been saying something I hadn't heard. 'Surely you can't *not* want to sell and cash in on the offer?'

'No,' I said slowly. 'It certainly seems the sensible thing to do.'

'But.' Rochelle said it flatly. 'There is a "but" somewhere. Why on earth? What's Selbridge Furniture to you?'

'Nothing,' I agreed. 'But – as you say, there is a "but". Not very logical, pehaps. You see, I was just wondering what Aunt Agnes would think.'

'The one who left you the shares?'

I nodded. 'She wasn't a blood relation. She was married to my father's Uncle Richard. They married late in life and had no children, and all her family were in Queensland, and I guess that was the reason she always made rather a fuss of my sister and me. And I thought she was terrific. I still think so. She helped her brother George found Selbridge Furniture – oh, in the late nineteen-twenties – and worked with him to get it established and helped hang on to it through the Depression. She always kept an interest in it – financial and otherwise. In her will she left my sister some money and she left me her share of the furniture business. According to the solicitor the idea was that it would return me an income.'

'But instead the company fell on hard times,' Rochelle said. 'Well, small businesses go to the wall in droves. If your aunt, or great-aunt, was a businesswoman it seems to me she'd certainly have cashed in her chips when she could. Sell when opportunity knocks. It mightn't come to the door again.'

I smiled. 'She helped hang on to it through the Depression, when things were much worse than they are now. That company meant a lot to her. That's why she never sold out her share to the other family partners.'

I kicked off my wet shoes. 'Did you say you're off to Perth for a year? That's great. I mean for you. You're on the way up and you deserve it. But that settles something for me: I'll let this flat go. I'm going up to Queensland to check out the company's position and meet the Selbridges before I decide how to vote. I think I owe Aunt Agnes that much.'

'Do you know any of the family?'

I shook my head. 'Aunt Agnes didn't talk very much about them as I remember. But of course, she had a stroke and lost her memory and spent her last couple of years in a nursing-home. I always went to visit her at weekends and once a Mrs Selbridge came down from Queensland to visit her, but I met her only once.'

I smiled a little. 'I do have one vivid memory of something Aunt Agnes did tell me once. She said: "Your cousin Julian's the pick of the lot of them. Julian West. Looks, brains, charm – he's what we'd have called *dashing* when I was young. Heaven knows what they call it now. They say he's a spend-thrift." '

I paused, remembering her chuckle and the mischievous gleam in her eyes.

'Then she added: "So he may be. I only know if I'd been forty years younger Eleanor wouldn't have got him." '

'Who's Eleanor?' asked Rochelle.

'She was a Selbridge. Julian isn't really my cousin, only married to one. And, if it comes to that, the Selbridges aren't really my cousins, either. They're not actually related to me – I'm only a connecion through Aunt Agnes's marriage to my father's uncle. I dare say they were none too pleased to find an outsider suddenly had a partnership in their business.'

'It must be a bit funny,' Rochelle agreed musingly. 'Must seem odd to you, too, doesn't it? I mean, a partnership in a business you know nothing about, and with partners you've never even seen.'

'Yes,' I said slowly. 'I don't think I've ever really thought about it before. It was just some vague thing which would be rather nice if it ever returned me any money, but I've certainly never thought of being anything but a sleeping partner. But now it's a bit different.'

'Julian sounds fun,' Rochelle said, suddenly sitting up and looking interested. 'Have you got any photographs of any of them? The Selbridge clan, I mean?'

'Yes, I believe I have. When Aunt Agnes died I had to go through her things, and there was a big envelope with snapshots of people. I didn't really look through them, but I should imagine some of them would be family.'

I got up and rummaged in a drawer and found the envelope and emptied its contents on the table. 'Of course, as I said, I met a Mrs Selbridge at the nursing-home once – she'd have been one of the furniture people I guess. Probably the redoubtable Julian's mother-in-law. I remember her as a small, well-groomed lady who would have been in her fifties, I suppose.'

Some of the photographs were quite old and in various stages of fading. Some were modern colour prints, and one of these was of a youngish couple posed outside a church – evidently a wedding photograph, though the young woman was dressed, not as a bride, but in a simple dress of soft blue. On the back was written: 'Eleanor and Julian.'

I stood looking at the snapshot for what might have been an unusually long time, a strange almost prickling sensation running through me which, even with the magical benefit of hindsight, I would hesitate to describe as any kind of premonition.

But there was something about Julian West which snatched and held the attention. It was even something much more than his good looks.

He would have been probably in his middle to late thirties when the photograph was taken. Dressed in an immaculate dove-grey suit, he had fair hair and moustache and blue eyes, and there was laughter in his face.

'Wow! Who's that?' Rochelle asked over my shoulder.

'Julian. Julian West. And Eleanor, of course.'

'He's quite a looker. So's she, for that matter. Pity she saw him first. But she looks like once she saw him she never saw anyone else.'

Rochelle was right: the photo showed Eleanor's face, tilted as she looked up at Julian, alight with joy. She was about twenty-seven, a tall, slender young woman who, like her husband, was fair-haired and blue-eyed, and she was almost beautiful.

'How come she's not dressed as a bride?' Rochelle demanded.

'I'm not sure. I have an idea she was married before – can't recall whether she was divorced or widowed.'

Rochelle was shuffling through the other photographs. 'Isn't it maddening? All these pictures of people, and hardly a name written on them, so we could be looking at some of your family-connections-cum-business-partners and we don't even know. Oh, hello, here's Eleanor again, so this must be the first husband – not a patch on the second.'

A younger Eleanor in traditional white, outside a different church and on the arm of a man some ten or fifteen years older, dark-haired and expensively suited but certainly lacking the good looks of his successor – though, as that thought ran through my head, it also occurred to me that he might be a good deal more comfortable to live with.

Eleanor hadn't lived with him for long. Paper-clipped to the back of the wedding photograph was a six-year-old newspaper cutting bearing a picture of the same man:

'Peter De Witt, founder of the Sunlink chain of motels, was killed yesterday when his late-model sedan crashed into a tree after it is believed it struck an oil-slick on the Bruce Highway south of Maryborough.'

Rochelle read it. 'Well, you're learning something about the family. How many others are there?'

'There are four involved in the furniture business: Rachael Selbridge, who I presume is the lady who came to see Aunt Agnes; and her three children – she's a widow. She was married to Aunt Agnes's brother George's son – his only child, in fact. Apart from Eleanor I know nothing about Rachael Selbridge's children except their names: Gordon and Nigel.'

'So it's a tight little family group except for you.' She frowned a little in concentration. 'I wish I could remember why the name Selbridge stuck in my mind. I'm sure there was some crime – an unusual one. You know, Trisha, you really might not be awfully welcome if you do go up there poking around their nice little family business to see what makes it tick – or fail to tick, if that's the case. They really might not love their long-lost cousin-of-a-sort at all.'

'No,' I said slowly. 'No, I suppose they really might not.' I picked up the letter again. 'There's no hint of what the family feeling is concerning the take-over offer – no advice to sell or not to sell. All I'm sure of is that Aunt Agnes would have voted against selling, and it's her share I have. I owe it to her to go and look into the business till I can make some kind of an informed decision.'

I picked up my wet shoes and headed for the bedroom. 'Love me or hate me, the Selbridges are going to have to put up with me. Let's hope at least the sun is shining.'

Two

The sun was in fact shining warm and brilliant as I stopped at a motel on the outskirts of town and went in to book a room. The town lay in a hollow among folded hills, and as I'd approached it after the drive of something like an hour and a half from Brisbane I'd had glimpses of neat fields of silver-grey pineapples and, to the west, an impression of a green, fairly thickly-settled rolling valley and, beyond, the line of a low mountain range.

I asked the woman at the motel desk how I would find Selbridges' furniture factory. She gave me directions and added, 'You'll recognize it when you see it. They always keep the place looking nice – shrubs and lawns and things.'

She was right, I reflected as I parked the car outside the brick and timber building which was set in quite spacious and attractive grounds in a part of the town which was now a light-industrial estate but which no doubt had been virtually open land when the original Selbridge established his workshop. The building was in good repair and with reasonably freshly painted woodwork, the lawns were well cut and the blend of native and exotic trees and shrubs was appealing and spoke of pride of ownership. If Selbridge Furniture had encountered hard times, it wasn't apparent, and that in itself, I reflected, was good business practice.

As I walked up the path to the door marked 'Office' I realized that this was no large factory churning out mass-produced stuff. There was the spasmodic rip of a power-saw through timber, and various other sounds I couldn't identify, but it was all rather low-key.

A young woman at a typewriter was the sole occupant of the office and she looked up as I walked in. 'Can I help you?'

There was a door, evidently to an inner ofice, marked 'Manager: G.Selbridge', so I said, 'I'd like to see Mr Selbridge, please – Mr Gordon Selbridge.'

'I'm sorry, Mr Selbridge is out on lunch. Mr Weldon might be able to see you.'

'Who is Mr Weldon?' I enquired.

'He's the accountant, and in charge of sales, promotion, advertising – that sort of thing.'

'Sounds as if he's a busy man,' I said a trifle dryly.

She moved towards the the inner office. 'Who shall I say wishes to see him?'

I didn't particularly wish to see the multi-purpose Mr Weldon at all, but it seemed he would have to suffice for the moment. 'My name is Kent. Patricia Kent.'

The woman had opened the door to the second office as I spoke, and a man at a desk there looked up sharply and came to his feet.

'Miss Kent! Come in, please. I'm Martin Weldon.'

He came forward as he spoke, a man of about thirty, of medium height and the build and sun-tan of an athlete. 'What a delightful surprise.'

Lively brown eyes met mine in a smile, and I felt his welcome was real: Martin Weldon was pleased to see me. I wondered fleetingly why.

He drew up a chair for me and sat down again behind his desk. The main office was a reasonably large room, equipped with three desks and a drawing-board, and a second door opened, I guessed, into the factory area. The furnishings were superb for a modest business; obviously the office was planned to serve as an indication to prospective customers that Selbridges knew what good furniture was.

Martin Weldon said nothing for a minute, but just sat silently watching me with those alert dark eyes. I became aware of it and looked at him with an apologetic smile.

'I'm sorry. I was lost in thought. Is this Selbridge furniture? Forgive me, but it's rather more than average office furniture.'

He smiled. 'All Selbridge furniture is rather more than average. It used not to be, as I understand it. But Gordon – Gordon Selbridge – realized some years ago that for a small manufacturer to survive in a fiercely competitive field it had to concentrate on top quality. It couldn't hope to compete on the mass market.'

'He was probably right,' I said. 'But it doesn't seem to have worked very well, does it?'

'It was working before – well, before the company lost its funds. It can work again. It only needs time. It takes time for top-quality furniture to get established in the market. The company *can* survive – and prosper. It doesn't have to be sold.'

His eager enthusiasm took me by surprise, as did the reference to the company losing its funds. 'Will it be sold?' I asked.

He took a breath to say something and then hesitated. 'That's a matter for you and the other partners to decide. But no doubt you know their feelings. They are your cousins, I believe.'

'Not really. Only connected by marriage. And I don't know their feelings at all. Do they want to sell?'

'I believe there's a difference of opinion.'

He was treading warily, I thought: he knew exactly what they wanted to do and he wasn't going to talk about it.

'You don't want the company sold,' I said. 'Why not?'

White teeth flashed under a clipped black moustache as he smiled. 'You think I hardly fit the role of faithful old retainer. True. I've been here only about two years. Of course, I'd like to keep my job. But there's something a little more than that. I've become interested in the company, and I suppose there's some sort of personal pride involved. I'm in charge of sales promotion; when I said the company needed time to become known, what I really meant was that

I need time to make it known, and I'm certain I can do it. I'm selfish enough to want a real chance to try. It's – a challenge, that's all. I like a challenge.'

Looking at him, I could believe it.

'So you see, it's just a big ego thing with me, absolutely nothing noble or altruistic, I'm sorry to say.'

I could believe that, too. This was a fiercely practical man; an ambitious man who would never be content to be an employee all his life. I wondered if he had hopes of being able to buy into Selbridges as a partner, and I felt the company might do worse than accept him.

He said, 'Miss Kent, pardon my curiosity, but I had the impression that as you lived in Melbourne, and were something in the nature of a sleeping partner in Selbridges, you were expected to register your opinion on the sale of the company by letter. What made you decide to come here?'

'I'd thrown in my job and was at a loose end. But primarily I came because I inherited my share of Selbridges from an aunt who, I'm certain, wouldn't have been agreeable to accept any take-over offer, unless there was no other way out. I felt I owed it to her to come here and see the situation for myself, so that I could at least make some kind of an informed decision. No business venture is purely figures on a balance sheet.'

Martin Weldon was studying me keenly. 'It's very interesting that you should say that. I'd be most happy, of course, to show you the company books so that you can see the exact financial situation. For the rest, you must look over the factory and talk to your partners, of course. And, please, if I may ask you one thing: take time to think it all out. The decision doesn't have to be made for another week yet.'

The door from the outer office opened and a man said, 'Miss Kent, how good of you to come. Mrs Robinson told me you were here – sorry I was out. I'm Gordon Selbridge.'

He held out his hand with a smile – a tallish man in his middle thirties, with brown hair beginning prematurely to grey, and blue eyes behind dark-rimmed glasses.

This was the man who had decided Selbridge furniture had to be exclusive to survive, according to Martin Weldon. He looked like a man very capable of making decisions and sticking to them. I wonderd whether he wished to keep his company and meet the challenge of following up his policies in the same way his accountant-cum-sales-manager did.

We chatted generalities for a while, and he refused to hear of me staying at a motel, and insisted on personally phoning to cancel my room reservation.

'You must stay with us. I'll show you the way out to our place now, if you like – it's about five kilometres out of town. Or do you want to get straight down to business? Nigel's the best one to show you over the factory; he's the designer of all our stuff, but he's away in Brisbane today. Or Martin can show you the books and let you check out our present financial position.'

I smiled. 'I have to start somewhere, sometime. That's why I'm here. I'll do the dull bit first and check the books. But are you sure it's convenient for me to stay with you?'

'Of course. Christine – my wife – will be happy to have you stay. It's a big house with plenty of room, even apart from Eleanor's flat.'

I blinked. Eleanor's flat. I realized fully for the first time that I had walked into the life of a family I knew nothing about, and if as Martin Weldon had suggested there were divisions within the family over whether or not to sell the company, I should have to take sides. I was going to become involved with these people, perhaps earn the enmity of some simply because I *had* to take sides by taking a stance for or against selling. For a moment I wished Aunt Agnes had never left me her share of Selbridge Furniture.

I spent a couple of hours studying the financial status of the company and its trading over the past two years. It had been heavily in debt. It had been getting an increasing share of orders, and it had traded itself almost out of debt and looked to me as if it could survive, though how well it could prosper I certainly couldn't forecast. I could also see why some of the family members might want to sell out.

Rachael Selbridge, Eleanor West and I, as non-active partners, were dependent on the company making profits before we received an income from it. Gordon and Nigel, who worked in the business full-time, naturally were entitled to a salary. Gordon's salary was a modest one indeed – the employed craftsmen made more than he did; Nigel's was startlingly almost non-existent. And as there had been no profits, Rachael, Eleanor and I had received nothing. It hadn't mattered to me because I'd had a good job and the idea of being a sleeping-partner in a furniture factory had been nothing more than a rather amusing novelty, and anyway I hadn't been a partner long enough to begin to look for dividends, pleasant though they would have been.

But Rachael at least might be in a very different position. I didn't know about Eleanor, though it seemed her first husband might have left her financially well situated; I didn't know what Julian West's occupation might be.

Any of them might be anxious to at least reap some financial benefits from Selbridge Furniture Company – by selling it.

'Suppose I take you home now,' Gordon's voice interrupted my thoughts. 'I've phoned Christine and she's expecting you for afternoon tea. Nigel will join us for dinner, and you can probably meet Eleanor, though I doubt she'll have dinner with us. And of course you must meet my mother – perhaps tomorrow. She has a unit at one of the local beach resorts. We'll leave any business talks until you've met us all.'

'Thank you. You've been most kind.' I hesitated. 'You spoke of Eleanor having a flat in your house.' It was half a question.

He shook his head. 'Not exactly. It's Eleanor's house. She has a small flat in part of it. Christine and I rent the rest of the house from her.'

'Oh,' I said. 'I see.'

I didn't, of course. A small flat in their own house, while they rented out the rest of it, seemed a strange situation for

Eleanor and Julian to be living in. However, there must be reasons, and I didn't feel I could begin asking questions about the family's private living arrangements.

I followed Gordon's car past residential areas and into farmland toward the foot of the bush-clad range, and sealed road gave way to gravel and presently he turned off and drove up to a tree-shaded house built in brick and timber in the colonial style, with deep verandas and, in spite of its obvious age, an air of solid comfort – a big, rambling house which belonged to another era but which fitted perfectly into its setting. The range behind it was not quite close enough to be oppressive and the outlook was over gently rolling hills with a glimpse of the town in the valley, and the soft green of cane-fields beyond. Bananas grew in plantation on a near slope, and a little farther away dairy cattle were stringing home from their pasture for afternoon milking and the quick yap of an attendant dog came on the clear winter air as I got out of the car.

A woman of about thirty, fair-haired and slightly plump, came out to greet us. 'It's so nice to meet you, Patricia,' she said, kissing my cheek with easy, unaffected warmth. 'Gordon will bring your things and I'll show you your room. I'll have afternoon tea ready in ten minutes – soon as you've freshened up. If you've been poring over accounts all afternoon you must be ready to have a cup of tea.'

We had afternoon tea in a pleasant, sun-warmed room. Clearly the house had been extensively – and expensively – renovated in fine taste, with clever use of wood-panelling in the warm tones of cedar mingled with light, cool-looking paintwork.

Gordon went back to work and Christine and I talked easily enough as we cleared away the tea things, but I felt she wanted to avoid any discussion on the reason for my being here, and any discussion on the family, except for talking of Aunt Agnes, whom Christine had known through her occasional visits to Queensland to visit the factory which had so long been part of her life.

Then the phone rang and Christine became involved in what seemed as if it might be a prolonged conversation so I took myself into the garden, which was pleasant, spacious and well tended. A bench against a sun-warmed stone wall was inviting, and I sat there looking out across the farmland which surrounded the house. The sun would soon disappear behind the western range, I noted as I sat relaxedly trying not to think too much about Selbridge Furniture. A handsome German shepherd dog came from somewhere and I didn't see it until it sniffed my hand and I jumped. But its intentions were purely friendly and it lay at my feet and I fondled its ears.

A rather tall woman, slender in grey slacks and a pink shirt that suited her fair hair came walking slowly up the drive, her head bent so that she didn't see me. I stood up as she came close and said, 'Good afternoon.'

She looked up swiftly and I recognized the woman in the two wedding snapshots Aunt Agnes had had, but I saw with a sense of pure shock that something – something cruel – had happened since that lively young woman had looked with laughing adoration at Julian West on the day she had married him.

Although that was only perhaps four years ago, she might have been twenty years older, her face drawn, eyes lacklustre, her mouth a bitter line. There was despair – grief– in everything about her, so strong that it was almost a tangible thing.

I said, 'You must be Mrs. West – Eleanor.'

She looked at me with open hostility. 'Who are you?' she demanded sharply.

'Patricia Kent – Trisha to my friends. I'm your Aunt Agnes's niece by marriage,' I added, as her immobile face suggested my name meant nothing. And suddenly I wondered whether anything had any meaning for Eleanor, because in spite of her quick question there was an air of remoteness about her.

'Why have you come here?' There was no less sharpness in the tone.

I said quietly, 'To see the business for myself before I made any decision on whether or not to vote to sell it. I thought I owed Aunt Agnes that much. Not that my vote will count for much, I dare say.'

'Haven't they told you?'

I shook my head. 'Told me what?'

She hadn't moved while we'd been speaking – not a turn of the head, a gesture of any kind. There was something unnerving about it.

'Oh, your vote will count all right,' she said. 'So you had better be sure you get it right, hadn't you?'

'I'm sorry, I don't think I understand.'

'We're a family divided, as you might say,' she said, and for the first time there was a hint of sardonic amusement in her voice. 'Two for. Two against. You have the casting vote.'

I stared. 'Oh, no,' I said flatly. I felt as if a dismaying weight had been settled on my shoulders, and what had begun as partly a kind of duty to an old lady I'd cared about, and partly just a diversion until I began looking for another job, had grown into something much bigger than I had wanted.

I gestured to the garden bench where I'd been sitting. 'Can we talk about it?'

The momentary flicker of life that had showed in Eleanor's face had gone, leaving only a blank indifference. 'The others can tell you everything,' she said.

'But I need to know so much,' I protested. 'Especially if there's a difference of opinion. The business has been in your family for three generations. I should think there'd be a good deal of anguish at the thought of selling.'

'Anguish.'

She said the word almost softly, yet with a controlled violence that was as startling as if she had screamed. She looked at me with contempt ice-hard in her eyes. 'What do *you* know of our anguish?'

And she turned and walked into the house.

I sat down again slowly on the bench. The dog lifted her head and thumped her tail on the grass as she looked in the direction Eleanor had gone, but made no move to follow her.

'What,' I said aloud to my canine companion, 'has happened in this house? And where is Julian?'

'You could,' said a man behind me, 'try South America.'

I jumped and whirled around. My first embarrassed thought – that it was Julian West himself – was at once dispelled: this was not the handsome man in the photograph. He was a pleasant-looking fellow, but not handsome and certainly not what Aunt Agnes would have described as dashing. He was fairly tall, with mouse-brown hair and hazel eyes and, although he was dressed in a perfectly good business suit, he managed to look slightly rumpled and I felt he always would.

'Hello, Particia. I'm Nigel. Christine told me you were out here somewhere. I see you've met Tessa.' He stooped and patted the dog. 'And Eleanor.'

He sat down on the bench beside me and stretched out his long legs. 'Try not to mind Eleanor. She keeps very much to herself these days.' He glanced toward the house, and there was sympathy in his face.

Then he looked at me. 'I'm glad you thought enough of Aunt Agnes to take the trouble to come and look at the business for yourself. We were all very fond of her, too.'

'I'm beginning to wish,' I said ruefully, 'I hadn't come. Eleanor just told me the rest of you are equally divided on selling or not selling. I'll have the casting vote. That shouldn't be! How can I make a decision like that?'

He ran his eyes searchingly over my face. 'Rather a pity you know that it's up to you. Did Eleanor tell you who-wants-what course of action?'

I shook my head.

'Good. Gordon and I have talked about it – I dropped in at the factory on the way home from Brisbane, and then, consumed with natural curiosity, I came out to see you. Also, we've spoken with Mother on the phone, and I'll have a word with Eleanor. We've decided not to tell you what we want to do, but to let you make up your own mind independently. No one is going to pressure you one way or the other.'

'Martin Weldon wants to carry on business as usual,' I said. 'He's sure the business can survive and sales improve.'

Nigel smiled. 'Martin is a natural enthusiast.'

'He just might be right. At least I found his enthusiasm interesting.'

Nigel didn't answer and I said quickly, 'I'm sorry. That sounded as if I were trying to find out what you think, and I realize you're all trying to be fair by not influencing me.'

I turned my head to look directly at him. 'What did you mean when you said Julian might be in South America?'

He said wryly, 'I believe at least some South American countries don't allow extradition.'

'Extradition! Why would our police want to extradite Julian West?'

'For murder. Or at least attempted murder, which is the same thing but for a trick of fate.'

Three

'Murder!' I was staring at him in shock. 'But – who?'

He rubbed a foot absently against Tessa's back as the big dog stretched out enjoying the late sun. 'You don't really know anything about us, do you?'

'Not – no, I suppose I don't. I know Eleanor was maried to Peter De Witt and he was killed, and she later married Julian. Aunt Agnes,' I added almost defensively, 'thought Julian was wonderful.'

'Yes. At least she was spared knowing what happened.'

He stopped and seemed intent on rubbing Tessa's back.

'Are you going to tell me what happened?' I asked. 'I have to know some time.'

He nodded. 'Yes, of course. It's no secret. I was wondering where to begin. You see, when my father died the company was in some financial trouble. I'd just come back from doing an army stint in Vietnam and I probably wasn't being much help to anyone – rather hell-bent on living it up a bit and not too interested in the family business because I'd just finished a degree in architecture before I got drafted – had my call-up deferred till I got through.'

'You're an architect? Why are you working in a furniture factory? Sorry,' I added quickly. 'That's not my affair.'

'Oh, there's no mystery. My father was the designer of our furniture. Gordon had done a full apprenticeship under Dad, and also took a degree in business management; he's a pretty wide-awake fellow, but no designer. At that time we had a second branch of the business in a Brisbane suburb

and Gordon was the manager of that. Unfortunately that
branch proved an over-expansion of the business and things
weren't going well. Then Dad was killed in a boating
accident.'

'I'm sorry,' I said lamely. 'I didn't know that.'

'He loved to sail and had a small catamaran. He took it
out one day – alone, as he usually did – when conditions
weren't good enough. A bit of rough weather only looked
like a challenge to him, and he'd often scared Mother half to
death by going out in defiance of a bad-weather forecast.
He'd only laugh about it. But this time the sea was too good
for him. The catamaran was wrecked and he was drowned.'

'I'm sorry,' I said again, feeling inadequate.

He was silent for a little while. 'Yes. Well, that meant the
company had no designer, so as I hadn't yet set up as an
architect, I came in to design furniture instead of buildings.'

He smiled a little. 'I must admit I've found it much more
interesting – and challenging – than I expected. Especially
after Gordon insisted we make only really top-flight stuff.'

He put his hands behind his head and leaned back, gazing
lazily out over the countryside and looking as if he wasn't
really the type to care very much for challenges.

'Julian,' he went on, 'was the accountant then. He was
married to Eleanor, who had made over half her money to
him when they were married. She was left very comfortably
off by Peter, her first husband, but when Julian came along
she said she couldn't bear the thought of him being
relatively hard-up while she had a small fortune. She bought
this old house just before she and Julian were married, and
they had it extensively remodelled and redecorated while
they were overseas on a three-month honeymoon. Which
Eleanor paid for, of course. Julian had a lot to do with
planning the restoration and general refurbishing, and he
certainly had enough artistic sense to have it done very well
indeed, as you'll realize if you've seen inside.'

I nodded. 'It's rather beautiful'

'Eleanor began to have trouble in sleeping and was

prescribed some sleeping-tablets. She and Julian must have been married for – oh, eighteen months, I suppose. Julian said he thought she was nervous at night, and that was why she couldn't sleep, so he had security window bars and steel mesh doors put on, since the house is low-set. Julian was often out at night – working late, Rotary Club meetings and things like that – and although they employed an elderly couple to help in the house and garden their room was on the opposite side of the house from Eleanor and Julian's room, and Eleanor probably did feel somewhat alone in the house when Julian was out – after all, it's a big house, and of course Gordon and Christine weren't living here then.'

He paused and looked towards the house, his face troubled.

'It was a night in spring almost two years ago. Julian said he was going to visit some people who live – oh, a couple of kilometres down the road. Something to do with a Rotary project. He was a fitness fanatic so no one thought it odd when he said he'd walk instead of bothering to take the car, even though there was a storm brewing – be glad to get a breath of fresh air, he said, as it had been a hot day. Eleanor said she was feeling tired and wanted to go to bed early. The Marshes – the elderly couple – watched television for a while and decided they'd also have an early night, as they usually did, I believe. They hadn't long been asleep when the storm hit and Mrs Marsh was wakened by the howling wind and the rain and she said there was a most terrific crack of thunder. She got up to close their bedroom window, and she smelled smoke.

'At first, she said, she assumed it was from somewhere else, being blown in on the wind, but she began to check through the house because the smell of the smoke was quite strong. When she went to check on the far side of the house she saw a glow in the garden and realized it was being thrown through one of the windows from a fire inside the house.'

'Eleanor's room.' I said, feeling suddenly cold as I began to understand.

'Yes,' he said, and went on, not looking at me but off into some dark distance:

'Mrs Marsh began to scream to her husband to come, but he was a bit deaf and the storm was making the devil of a noise. Mrs Marsh ran to Eleanor's door and tried to open it, shouting at Eleanor to wake up. The door wouldn't open. Mrs Marsh thought it was jammed, because Eleanor never locked it although there was always a key in the inside lock. But then she said she realized the door *was* locked. There was no sound from Eleanor and Arthur Marsh still hadn't heard her calls for help.'

I had a sick feeling in my stomach as I mentally pictured the frantic woman beating on the door and screaming to two people who didn't hear her, while the fire inside the room grew hungrily, licking up the curtains and clawing for bedclothes.

'Thank God,' Nigel went on, 'Mrs Marsh kept her head. Even if Arthur had heard at once they'd have been hard-pressed to break the door down – all the doors in the house are solid oak and the locks are built to last; they'd have needed an axe, and by that time it would have been much too late. But she remembered a bunch of keys in a kitchen drawer – said she'd once asked Eleanor what they were, and Eleanor said they were duplicate keys to all the doors in the house. Mrs Marsh ran for the keys just as Arthur finally appeared on the scene and she screamed at him to call the fire brigade and ambulance.

'She said afterwards her hands were shaking so much she thought she'd never find the right key or be able to get it in the lock, but she did, and quickly. The door opened at once and they both ran into the room and somehow between them they managed to get Eleanor out – quite unconscious. Fortunately Arthur had been in the Navy in World War Two and had served as a medical orderly, so he not only had training in dealing with fires, he knew first aid. He slammed the door shut again as soon as they got Eleanor out, and that helped to contain the fire by shutting off the air, as the window was already closed – which was the only reason the fire hadn't got a hopeless hold earlier – it had needed more air.

'Then they carried Eleanor outside and he checked that she was breathing, and laid her with her head tilted slightly back to keep the air-passages open, and then he ran back into the house and grabbed a fire-extinguisher – which, incidentally, had been bought only after he himself had kept insisting there should be at least one – and did what he could with that. It wasn't nearly enough, but it slowed the fire a bit, and the brigade arrived very smartly and they were able to contain the fire to that one room.'

I looked at the house. 'It was a pretty plucky thing the Marshes did – to go into a burning room.'

He nodded. 'They each received an official recognition of their bravery. They were entitled to it, in my opinion. When Eleanor recovered she bought them a cottage to retire in.'

I said slowly, 'If it hadn't been for the storm waking Mrs Marsh Eleanor would have died.'

'Oh, yes. No question of it. Makes you wonder about an act of God. They might all have died – the Marshes, too. I've often wondered if Julian ever thought of that.'

'Julian!' The word was jerked out of me.

He looked at me curiously. 'What do you think I've been talking about? An accident?'

'No.' I gave a little shudder. 'No, I knew what you were saying. But just for a moment – thinking of it – I forgot. It's rather hard to believe anyone could be so – evil.'

A school bus came up the road and stopped at the driveway and Tessa instantly leapt to her feet and trotted off to meet the two children who got off the bus. A girl and boy, about ten and seven respectively, greeted the dog with enthusiasm, waved to us – eyeing me with interest, and went into the house.

'Wendy and Ken. Gordon and Christine's children,' Nigel said in explanation. 'Nice kids.'

'Do they know what happened here?'

'Oh, yes. I don't think it made a great impact on them, although it's rather hard to tell. They liked Julian's happy-go-lucky manner, and they were always fond of Eleanor. I think Kenny, particularly, finds it hard that she doesn't want to play games with them any more.'

I looked at him quickly, startled. 'It's as bad as that?'

'Oh, yes.' His voice was bitter. 'Eleanor has a couple of rooms in her own house. She seldom leaves them except to go for a walk across the paddocks where she feels she won't meet anyone. My sister was an attractive girl, clever, talented, full of laughter. Now she is a shattered, embittered recluse who avoids the world – her family included as much as possible – at thirty-two years old. I hope I never meet up with the bastard who did that to her. I'd kill him, and God knows he's not worth doing time for.'

After a little silence I said, 'She must have loved him very much.'

'She loved Peter, her first husband,' Nigel said, 'and when he was killed she was hit very hard. But Julian – Julian was the sun, moon, stars. Julian was the hub of her world. If he had died it would have been bad enough, but to do what he did –' He stopped and shook his head.

'How did he set it up?' I asked. 'And why? You said she'd already given him half her money.'

'Yes. But half wasn't enough. Not for Julian. How he went through as much as he did, no one knows. He speculated on the Stock Exchange in a fairly big way, and apparently he was the proverbial big-spender in everything he did. The money Eleanor had given him was gone – wherever it went – though no one knew that until the police began investigating. But that hadn't been enough, either. He'd also managed very cleverly to swindle our company for rather a lot of money – enough, anyway, to come within a whisker of destroying it.'

He gave a rueful smile. 'And he was clever enough to make it appear that, although both he and I were in the position to siphon the company income off for our own use,

I was the more likely to be the one who'd done it.'

'You? But it was your own company!'

'Only a share of it.'

'But your family would never have believed it was you.'

He shrugged. 'It's been known to happen in families – one member stealing from the others,' he said. 'And they'd have found it very hard to believe it was Julian. I was going through that let's-live-it-up-while-we-can burst I mentioned. It included gambling, which worried the family. I never gambled for big stakes, but no one could know that. Maybe Julian thought he could repay the money before the axe fell or the auditors found certain interesting discrepancies. Maybe I was only to be the scapegoat if an emergency arose.'

'What made anyone first suspect the fire wasn't an accident?'

'Well, the ambulance raced Eleanor to the hospital still unconscious, and everyone thought it was from smoke inhalation and the toxic gases a fire creates. But a pretty smart doctor picked up a clue at once that there was something else. She'd had an overdose of her sleeping tablets – not enough to kill, but certainly enough to make her unconscious. There was evidence the fire had started in a waste-paper basket beside the bedside table. An ashtray had been knocked into it and presumably it would have appeared a cigarette-butt had started the fire. Eleanor doesn't smoke now, but she did then. There were long curtains beside the waste-paper basket. One assumes Julian made sure there was extra paper in the basket and a match or a cigarette-lighter was used to make sure the fire got properly started, although if the house had burned down and Eleanor had died, it would have appeared no more than a tragic accident.

'Julian could have come back half an hour later and been the perfect grieving husband and everyone would have shaken his hand sympathetically and he'd have collected the house and the rest of Eleanor's money. And mind you, he might not have spent the first half of it: all anyone knows is that it disappeared out of his bank account. It may have turned up in another account in another place and in another name. It may be that once he got that money he'd have paid back what he'd swindled from the company, or it may be that he'd have left me to take the blame.'

'But his plan went wrong,' I said.

Nigel nodded. 'He no doubt waited and watched from a safe distance. The people he'd said he was going to visit were out, but if things had gone his way the house would have been hopelessly ablaze long before he'd have had time to get to their house and back.'

'Did the Marshes know if he'd ever really left this house? Surely he'd have taken an awful risk to go out and come back? They might have seen him.'

'Yes. That was the hope that Eleanor clung to at first: that it wasn't possible. It must have been very risky indeed – must have needed an awful lot of nerve and a bit of luck for him to get back to the bedroom unobserved. He did leave the house. Arthur Marsh saw him walk down the driveway – in fact, he called Arthur out to discuss a tree in the garden which he thought should be lopped. It was almost certainly a deliberate ploy to have a witness to the fact he had indeed left the house before Eleanor went to bed. In order to get back into the bedroom – and out again – he would have had to walk down the hall past the room where the Marshes were sitting watching telelvision.'

'Suppose they'd seen him?'

'There wasn't as much risk, I suppose, as you'd think at first. They'd be sitting in easy-chairs with their backs turned to the doorway, so if he was quiet the odds were his way. And if they'd seen him – well, I'm sure he'd have had an explanation ready and plausible. It would have meant he'd have had to postpone it all till another time, but presumably that would merely have been an inconvenience.'

'Why couldn't he have got in and out by a bedroom window?'

'He'd had security bars put on the windows. Ostensibly to soothe Eleanor's nerves by guaranteeing no intruder could get in. They also guaranteed no one trapped by a fire and a locked door could get out. And they gave him an alibi, at least of a sort.'

He shrugged. 'As I said: he had nerve. And luck.'

'But his luck ran out.'

'Yes. He'd have seen the ambulance and fire engine; seen the fire die down and go out, seen the ambulance tear off with siren screaming, telling him they were carrying a live woman who might be saved, not a dead body which had left him a handsome inheritance. He must have realized there was virtually no chance now that his scheme wouldn't be found out. The game was up. So he made a run for it. I must say he did it very well. There was a pretty wide police search, but he'd got clear away.'

There was a silence while my brain was struggling to absorb the situation.

'How was it thought he gave Eleanor the overdose?' I asked.

Perhaps there was something still doubting in my tone, for he gave me an odd sideways look.

'You'd like to think it was all a horrible mistake, wouldn't you?' he asked. 'Aunt Agnes's favourite nephew exonerated?'

I shook my head. 'No. Well, yes, I suppose I would. I'd rather not think anyone would be so rotten.'

He gave a short laugh. 'Oh, plenty of people are quite capable of such things. Read the newspapers sometime – or if you don't trust the newspapers try reading history. You won't run short of evidence of human rottenness.'

From inside the house there was the sound of one of the children laughing. Coming just at that moment, it seemed both incongruous and reassuring.

'I'm sorry,' I said, and added grimly, 'if it's hard for *me* to accept – never having even seen the man – how must it have been for Eleanor?'

He nodded. 'It's assumed he put the sleeping-tablets, no doubt crushed, into a spicy sort of chicken dish he'd suggested to Eleanor she make for dinner. He served it and brought it to the table. Even by the time dinner was over Eleanor was complaining of being extraordinarily tired, and Julian suggested she go to bed and he and Mrs Marsh would wash up. The thoughtful husband to the end.'

He tapped at the ground with the heel of his boot. 'He had carefully planned to ensure no suspicion could fall on him, because from the time they had dinner until he walked down the driveway on his way to visit his friends, he was never out of sight of one or other of the Marshes. He must then have doubled back, and re-entered the house. The Marshes were watching television, Eleanor by then would have succumbed to the sleeping-pills, and he could go into the bedroom, set the fire, lock the door, take the key and slip out again.'

'How could everyone be sure the door to the bedroom really *had* been locked?'

'There was always a key in the lock on the inside of the door. After the fire, although the door was not damaged, the key was not in the lock and a meticulous search by the police – and by Eleanor herself – failed to find it in the room anywhere. Plus the fact that Mrs Marsh couldn't open the door until she got the spare key, and then it opened at once. And of course, there was the one overwhelming thing that pointed to Julian's guilt.'

'He ran away,' I said.

'Yes.' Nigel stretched out his legs and looked hard at his boots as if he found them interesting.

'At first,' he said, 'Eleanor flatly refused to believe her beloved Julian had tried to kill her. It was all an accident, she vowed. She must have forgotten she'd taken her sleeping-pills and had taken more, then in her sleepy state had knocked the ashtray into the wastepaper basket without noticing. As for Julian's disappearance – something had happened to him, perhaps an accident. She insisted on search parties combing the paddocks near the road. As time went on and he wasn't found, she said he had suffered amnesia; he must have; he would come back. But eventually, when they showed her the evidence of the disappearance of money from his bank account, the embezzlement of the company funds – and he didn't come back – she had to accept the truth. And she went into her room and shut the door and to all intents and purposes she never came out again.

'The company was so close to ruin, so heavily in debt, that the branch Gordon was managing in Brisbane had to be closed, and it was only in rented premises, so there was nothing in the way of assets to sell to help get us out of trouble. Gordon and Christine came back here and rented Eleanor's house, and we set to work to try to get the company back on its feet. When Martin Weldon came along – he'd been working as an accountant with another business-house here in town for a couple of years, I think – and asked for a position with the company, knowing Julian had once been our accountant, it seemed as if it might be worth the expense on an extra salary: he was full of bright ideas, enthusiasm. I must say he seems to stay that way.'

'He showed me the books this afternoon,' I said somewhat hesitantly. 'I'm not an accountant, but it seems to me the company has managed to trade itself out of its debts. Gordon has worked for a small salary considering his position. And you've worked for a pittance.'

He raised one eyebrow. 'I could have been the embezzler. I guess I had some kind of feeling that I wanted to be sure no one could say in the future I'd wrecked Selbridges. I wanted to pay the money back.'

'Even though it wasn't your debt?'

He looked at me with a lazily amused smile. 'Why are you so sure of that, I wonder?'

I met his steady hazel eyes for a moment and felt my face flush slightly, defensively. 'But obviously Julian – '

'Obviously Julian was a beast – no, that's an insult to the animal kingdom. It doesn't *prove* he was an embezzler. I – oh,

I don't know. I had some kind of fixation about it, I guess. A kind of rage that a tint of suspicion could fall on me.'

He grinned disarmingly. 'An insult to my noble name. Or sheer pig-headed arrogance. Or something equally silly. Anyway, it was something I had to do.'

'Pay back money you hadn't taken? What about Eleanor? She had plenty of money, so you say. Why could she have at least loaned the company money to get it out of trouble? It was her husband who'd taken it, after all.'

'No!' He said it sharply, violently, almost startling me with his vehemence. 'Eleanor had had enough.'

He got up. 'Come, it's getting chilly out here, and there's Gordon arriving home.'

A car turned into the drive. 'Let's go indoors.'

The evening was pleasant and friendly. Gordon was a lively conversationalist, an energetic, volatile man who was a contrast in personalities to his nonchalant, easy-going brother – which, I reflected, was probably the reason they could work together successfully. Christine was a placid, even-tempered girl who evidently devoted herself to making a career of being wife to Gordon and mother to the children, and at the same time I was sure she was alertly and intelligently aware of all that went on in the business. Gordon was obviously tremendously fond of her and I felt he was probably much more dependent on her than he realized.

The children were lively and cheerful without being intrusive – nice kids, as Nigel had said. There was no business discussion during the evening, and Eleanor did not join us for dinner.

When I was ready for bed I turned the light out and drew back the curtains and stood for a time looking out on to the starlit garden where shrubs and trees were no more than darker shapes against the grass, except where, farther along the line of the house wall, light from a window glowed softly, through curtains evidently, and I heard the sound of a

piano. Eleanor's room, I thought. At first I assumed the
music was a record-player or a radio, but presently I
realized it was someone actually playing in the house and I
listened with sharpened attention, for even though the
sound came to me only faintly it was obviously played with
much more than ordinary artistry. I hoped the tormented
Eleanor found some peace in playing.

I thought of the elderly housekeeper, that night nearly
two years ago, looking out on to the garden as I was doing
now, and seeing the glow, not of electric light but of fire.

I ran my hand, almost before I thought, around the frame
of my bedroom window. If there ever had been security bars
on this window they had been removed, and I was grateful.

Four

I woke early and went out into the garden as soon as I
dressed. I could hear the sound of children's voices and
went toward them, to find a tennis court with Wendy and
Ken energetically and with a degree of skill surprising for
their age, engaged in a game which was naturally going in
favour of Wendy in view of her advantage in age and height,
though her little brother seemed unperturbed and battled
manfully.

'Hello!' he panted when he saw me. 'Want a game?'

'Oh, you're both much too good for me,' I told him. 'I'm
just out for a walk. Is he yours?' I nodded at a grey horse
who was standing by the garden fence watching the young
protagonists on the court.

'Yes, that's Dobby,' Wendy said. 'He's waiting for us to
give him some hay before we go to school. Come on, Kenny,
we'd better.'

I went with them as they put their tennis racquets away in
the laundry and got a bundle of hay from a neat,
new-looking garden shed. 'How much land is yours?' I
asked.

'About a hectare,' Wendy said. 'Of course, it's not ours,
it's Aunt Eleanor's really. But she lets us do what we like
with it. That's how we have Dobby – that's short for
Dobbin,' she added.

'He's very nice,' I said, patting the patient nose and trying
to look as if I knew something about horses.

'Yes,' Ken agreed, handing out fistfuls of hay. 'He's an

Arab, of course, but he's pretty old. That's why he was cheap. Uncle Nigel bought him for us.'

'Did he now?' I said.

'Mum and Dad didn't have enough money,' Wendy explained with the candour of the very young. 'Of course, Dobby's nothing like as good as Mr Weldon's horses.'

'He is so!' Ken protested loyally. 'He's old, that's all.'

'Mr Weldon breeds quarter-horses,' Wendy went on.

'Really?' The interest in my tone was genuine.

'He's got a house and a sort of farm up on the range.' She nodded to the escarpment to the west. 'I wish we had a farm and lots of animals.'

'This used to be a farm once,' Ken said, 'a long time ago, when the house was first built. The people had an orchard and made brandy.'

'Not brandy, silly,' Wendy corrected firmly. 'Wine. And you call it a vineyard. But it wasn't any good because the grapes didn't grow properly. Aunt Eleanor told us once that the people used to make the wine in an old shed that used to be over there near the house. But they ploughed the grapes out a long time ago and Aunt Eleanor sold most of the land, and the old shed got blown down in a storm. Come on Ken, it's time we got ready for school.'

I lingered for a while watching Dobby munch his hay and wondering about the lazy-eyed man who had lived in near-poverty rather than endure the faintest suspicion that he had taken money from his family's company, and yet had managed to buy a horse for two children who wanted animals.

I turned and looked up to the steep rise of the range, mostly dark with scrub, but with some sweeping ridges of green pasture where cattle were dotted. And I thought of the athletic-looking Martin Weldon who owned, according to the children, a horse stud and a house. Martin had that kind of dynamic personality which told that here was a man who would get on in the world. There was *drive* – I couldn't think of any other word – in every line of him; and yet, too, there was a sparkle of laughter in those brown eyes which told that he would never let business dominate his life to the extent it would swamp his sense of fun and a liking for enjoying himself.

I looked over the surrounding farmland – dairy pastures, bananas and something I thought might be tomatoes – and thought of the early settler who had built this fine house and set up a winery. His dream had crumbled around him because he hadn't taken fully into consideration something as basic as the suitability of soil and climate for his venture.

Martin Weldon, I thought, would never make that kind of mistake. If he believed in Selbridge Furniture – believed enough, as I suspected, to hope to buy into a partnership one day – then I could believe also that Selbridges would survive and prosper. And yet, I told myself, I was being foolish; I didn't know the man well enough to be sure of any such thing – couldn't intelligently place such blind faith in his business acumen.

I would have to decide for myself.

The burden of that responsibility seemed suddenly to drop over me like a rain-sodden cloak. Today I had to go through the factory, see it in function, talk to the people who worked there, look at the product they created, and try – Heaven help everybody – to find the right answer. And in the end, of course, it would be right for me alone.

I sighed and went into the house.

No one attempted to show me around the factory. Nigel explained that the employees had been told who I was and why I was here, and they would answer any questions I liked to ask; but the family wanted me to see the business with entirely fresh eyes and without any suggestion of influence which anyone acting as guide might even unconsciously exert.

Gordon settled to paperwork at his desk and Nigel went to the high stool at his drawing-board and produced a notebook from his pocket which had some roughly-drawn lines, meaningless to me, and began studying it. I went through to the workrooms.

The factory was divided off into sections and I went slowly from one to another. A middle-aged woman working at an oversized sewing-machine was making chair-seat covers in a brocade-type material, piped and seamed with exquisite precision. Racks and rolls of furnishing fabrics of many kinds lined one wall, and a large cutting table was heaped with more of the material the woman was sewing.

I watched her work for a while and then she stopped her machine and smiled up at me, and explained her work, which was the cutting and sewing up of the materials which Nigel chose and to the patterns of his design. She had worked here, she said, for ten years since she and her husband had been divorced. She showed me the various materials – brocades and velvets, heavyweight linens and wools and tapestries; bold colours, gentle pastels, silky Regency stripes and tumbled masses of flowers caught morning-fresh forever in fabric – and I was told which were the easiest and which the most difficult to work with, and which had 'made up something beautiful' in a certain dining setting, and which had been completely made up once for a lounge suite and when Mr Nigel Selbridge saw it he ordered it all removed because it didn't look right on that particular design of divan.

I eventually moved on to talk to a large man who was attaching leather upholstery to an easy-chair, his strong hands deft and precise in their movements. He glanced up at me and nodded and simply went on working while I watched him. He was a man past middle-age, and I wondered how long he had done this sort of work. I asked.

He put down the little round-headed hammer with which he had been tapping home furniture-tacks on the underside of the chair-frame.

'Since I was sixteen,' he said. 'I did my apprenticeship under old Mr George Selbridge – Gordon and Nigel's grandfather. He founded the company, as you'll know –

him and his sister. I've been here over forty years – long before Gordon was born.'

'Do you ever get tired of the job?' I asked.

'Tired of it?' He looked startled, as if the thought had never occurred to him. He shook his head and ran his hand over the leather on the chair, lightly, almost as he might caress a woman. 'No. Sometimes I've wondered what I'll do when I retire. Wife says I'll probably make furniture for a hobby.' He grinned.

'Are you a cabinetmaker as well?'

'No. Just an upholsterer. Oh, I make the frames for the upholstered furniture.'

He walked over to a saw-bench and I followed. He picked up a piece of timber and held it out. 'See that?' He pointed to the end where neat slots had been sawn. 'You hear a lot about furniture these days being held together with glue and a few staples from a staple-gun. That doesn't happen here. Everything's dovetailed and morticed and dowelled and screwed as well as being glued. If anyone buys Selbridge furniture, they pay. But they get the best.'

There was pride in his voice and in the light blue eyes behind thick-lensed glasses.

'It wasn't always like that,' he added, and then, quickly: 'I don't mean the stuff was shoddy. But it was cheaper. The kind of furniture I can have in my house, if you like. When Henry died – George's son, father of Gordon and Nigel – Gordon realized very smartly that Selbridges couldn't hope to compete with big factories that turned out mass-produced stuff. I think he'd had a few arguments with Henry about it before as a matter of fact. Anyway, everything was changed. No more chipboard and laminated surfaces and imitation woodgrains and vinyls. Solid teak and rosewood and silky-oak and maple and walnut and so on. The best fabrics. Leather – real leather – and the best available.'

He picked up the dovetailed piece of timber again. 'Hardwood. Mountain ash. That's the sort of thing the

frames of our easy-chairs and sofas are made of. Cushions
hand-cut from top quality dacron and foam, and sealed in
calico to keep their shape. Some of our chairs in the antique
designs are even upholstered in real horsehair. Plenty of
tempered steel springs. It's not designed just to look good.
Nigel has spent a lot of time consulting with orthopaedic
specialists and chiropractors. He makes sure first our
furniture is good to use – comfortable and supporting. *Then*
he sets to work on its looks. And in the cabinet-making
section, two of the best tradesmen you'd find. Furniture for
people with enough money to buy the best, and enough
taste to recognize it.'

He paused. 'It sounds like snobbery. It isn't. It's just – just
a kind of good feeling that what you're producing is top
stuff, even if you could never afford to own it yourself.'

He shrugged and turned away abruptly to go back to
fitting the leather chair-cover. 'Sorry if I've bored you,' he
said almost gruffly.

'No,' I said quietly. 'I wasn't bored.'

Martin Weldon came in and asked if I'd like some lunch. I
glanced at my watch, startled to find how much time had
passed.

'I know a nice coffee shop where they serve a good light
lunch, and it's quiet.' He smiled as I hesitated. 'And I won't
mention furniture the entire time. Scout's honour.'

He was as good as his word. He talked about his horses
and his little property on the range behind the town. 'I like
to be out in the open air whenever I'm not in the office. So I
bought a house and a bit of land when there was something
of a boom in horses and just about anything with a mane
and four legs was fetching a good price, and I began
breeding quarter-horses. Alas, the boom is over.'

'Pardon my abysmal ignorance, but just what is a
quarter-horse?'

'A breed developed to run very fast over a short distance –
specifically for racing a quarter of a mile. Perhaps you'll
come riding one day.'

I laughed. 'I don't want anything that runs fast over any distance. All I know about horses is that they wear saddles and bridles and have a leg on each corner.'

'That's a start. You'd love them, I suspect. And quarter-horses have great manners – at least mine have.'

Somehow before lunch was over he extracted a promise that I would indeed go riding. Later I wondered at my recklessness. Since I'd never sat astride a horse in my life, something as innocuous as the children's old grey Dobby would have been somewhat more appropriate than something with the spirit to suit Martin Weldon.

After lunch I went into the cabinet-making section of the factory. The moment I stepped in two things caught my attention. The first was the smell of timber. I shall never know why, but something about that smell sent a prickle of excitement through my veins. It has been so ever since, whenever – anywhere – I catch the pungent scent of freshly-sawn timber.

The second thing to snatch at my attention was a young man in a wheelchair. In his middle to late twenties, thin, wiry and black-haired, he was intent on feeding a piece of pale-coloured timber into a machine which cut decorative grooves in it at his deft and precise manipulation. Then he spun his chair with the unthinking skill of long practice and wheeled swiftly to a bench where he measured and marked the strip of timber and, flicking a switch on an electric saw-bench, trimmed the ends at precise angles, so that I realized I was looking at the making of a frame for a glass-panelled door.

The young man looked up and met my eyes, his own dark ones glittering with resentment.

'Satisfied I'm capable of earning my keep? I'm not just a Selbridge charity project?' He spat the words at me with biting aggressiveness.

I blinked, startled. 'I was interested in what you were doing, that's all,' I said defensively. 'I don't know the first thing about furniture manufacture. I'm just here to look around, to – '

'Oh, sure, we've all been told. How to run a furniture factory in three easy lessons.'

He had turned his chair to face me, and was staring at me with a kind of hostile contempt that was so openly rude and unfair that I felt anger flare through me.

'You listen to me for a minute!' I snapped. 'I had a share in this business dropped in my lap. I didn't ask for it, I didn't want it. But I've got it and now I have to decide what to about it – what to do about this company. I might do the right thing or the wrong thing for quite a few people. At least give me credit for trying to get some basic idea of what the business is all about. All right?'

He looked at me for a moment, and then lifted one eyebrow. 'Well, well. A woman of spirit, it seems. Go ahead, watch what we do. What will it tell you?'

'I don't know,' I admitted. 'Maybe something.'

He turned back to the bench and began fitting the door-frame together.

'How long have you worked here?' I asked.

'A bit under two years.'

'How long have you been in a wheelchair?' I asked it bluntly, determined not to let him use his disability as an excuse for his rudeness. However much I might feel sorry for this young man, I felt if we were ever to regard each other cordially I must never show him an ounce of pity, because he would hate me for it.

'Five years.' He wheeled around to face me again. 'Oh, yes. They took me on in spite of the fact I was crippled. Bloody charitable of them, wasn't it?'

'If you're always as rude as this,' I told him calmly, 'it was more than charitable. It was bloody stupid.'

He gave a short laugh. 'I'm paid to work, not to have charming manners. And I work. I'm a good cabinetmaker.'

'I'm pleased to hear it. You'd certainly make a rotten butler. What will you do if the factory is bought out? Go on insulting the new owners?'

He laughed derisively. 'Good God, you don't really think the new owners would be employing any of us, do you?'

'Why not? If you're a good tradesman? The offer is for the place as a going concern. Why would they want to change the staff?'

'Change the staff.' He rolled his eyes heavenward. 'Listen, lady, it's no secret who wants to buy Selbridges. They're a big company. Their stuff might be as good as ours and it might not. But this is hardly an expansion move. Think, will you? Their factory's in Sydney. Their management's in Sydney. What would they want with a little company in a Queensland country town? It's the same old story with all the big boys in business. They don't want competition. They only buy up the little places to close 'em down.'

I stared at him. It was an idea which simply hadn't occurred to me, for some reason. Certainly no one else had mentioned it.

I stayed in the cabinet-making section for the rest of the afternoon, watching the craftsmen at work. I saw glass cut and fitted to door-panels. I saw the skills of French-polishing being applied to rosewood to bring its grain to glowing richness. I was introduced to jigsaws and band saws and routers and sanders and a host of other machines and tools which left me in total confusion but nonetheless fascinated me.

Keith Barnes, the bitter young paraplegic, didn't address another word to me except in answer to a direct question about a machine or a type of timber. I had never met a ruder person in my life, and yet I wondered whether that fierce discourtesy was deliberate – a barrier against the sympathy I felt he loathed and feared – or whether it was the result of a consuming rage against his disablement.

At five o'clock a young woman came into the section, a girl of perhaps twenty-five, shorter than average, slender, auburn-haired, with blue-grey eyes that twinkled with ever-ready laughter. She went to where Keith was packing away his tools and bent and kissed him.

'Hello, darling. I phoned the garage, but they're still waiting for that part for your car.'

He reached out and took her hand for a moment and smiled at her while I stared in near-disbelief at the change in his manner. 'I'll just go and wash up a bit,' he said, and wheeled away towards the men's room, checking just a moment to glance towards me. 'Oh, this is Patricia Kent. My wife Rhelma.'

The girl smiled at me. 'Hello. Have you been in the factory all day? Keith said they'd all been told you were going to spend a few days familiarizing yourself with the place. Have you found it – what? Interesting? Dull? Confusing?'

'Confusing, yes. But never dull.'

'Was Keith very awful to you? No,' she added quickly, 'you don't need to answer that.' Her face softened. 'Don't mind Keith, Patricia. His bad manners are just an act. He's not like that, truly. It's a kind of defence, I guess. He wants people to dislike him so that they won't pity him. That's the one thing he can't accept – pity.'

'What happened to him – an accident?'

She nodded. 'He'd been playing squash. He was driving home, and a car went through a red light. The driver got six months jail for being "under the influence of liquor or a drug" as the courts put it. Keith got life imprisonment in a wheelchair.'

He came back before I could think of anything intelligent to say, and they went out together, she walking beside his chair and making no move to assist him in anything, while they chatted easily, and I even heard him laugh.

I lay awake for a long time that night. I kept thinking of those three employees of Selbridges: Margery Long, the machinist-cutter; Otto Klein, so deeply involved with his upholstery work he didn't want to think of retirement; and the fierce young cabinetmaker. There were other employees, of course, but those were the three imprinted on my mind.

Because if the factory closed, none of them was likely to get other work – not in the depressed labour-market of the day.

How justified was Keith Barnes's prediction that the company which wanted to buy Selbridge Furniture would simply close the factory? Probably it was entirely correct. Yet if I voted to keep the company, *and it failed to survive* the economic pressures on it and went to the wall, its employees would be out of work anyway. And I would have left my partners with a defunct company and an empty factory instead of a fairly handsome share of the proffered purchase price.

There were still five days before the family had to hold their meeting to reach a decision on the purchase offer. I felt bitterly I would be no better qualified to reach a decision then than I was now.

Five

Two of those five days were a weekend, during which I had lunch with Rachael Selbridge and found her a quietly charming lady who, like the other members of the family, spoke with affection of my great-aunt Agnes and gave me no hint of how she intended to vote at the formal company meeting.

I also went riding with Martin and found his claims about the temperament of his horses were well justified, as was his prediction that I would love them. My mount patiently accepted my inept behaviour and never once took advantage of my hopeless inexperience. Martin showed me how he had taught Mindy, the bay mare he was riding, to go to him instantly at a call, even if she couldn't see him. He played a kind of hide-and-seek game with her which they both seemed to enjoy enormously. He could call her from behind the house, or out of sight in the stables, or on the far side of a clump of trees, and with excited little whinnies she would trot around until she found him, and would push her muzzle against his chest.

He had an attractively situated house on several hectares of land on the first shelf of the range that rose in two steps behind where Eleanor's house stood. The area was green with farmland and dotted with houses where other farms had been turned into large and pleasant residential blocks. Martin proved to be a delightful companion and the few hours I spent with him and his horses were a happy time in which I could forget Selbridge Furniture even existed.

I was still in a cheerful frame of mind on Monday morning when I went to the factory with Gordon and Nigel in Gordon's car. Otto Klein was just parking his car as we arrived, Martin was driving into the yard, and Keith Barnes had transferred himself – as I'd been told he was perfectly adept at doing unaided – from his now repaired specially equipped car to his wheelchair. As Gordon was unlocking the front door with some small joke about everyone arriving together, Keith said sharply, his voice cutting Gordon's to silence:

'The bloody place is on fire!'

I think there was perhaps one shocked second when no one moved. Then the first curls of black smoke oozing out of the building from under the roof registered with us all.

Gordon flung open the door. I don't know what I expected, but the place seemed incredibly normal: no flames, not even smoke in the office section. Only an acrid smell warned that something was wrong. It was the same in the main section of the building as some of us ran through, while behind us in the office I could hear Gordon phoning for the fire brigade, barely-controlled fear in his voice.

'It's in the stockroom!' I think it was Martin's voice from outside. Otto ran for a fire-extinguisher in a bracket on the wall and Nigel grabbed a length of cut calico lying on a bench – presumably to use as a beater. I remember saying: 'Be careful!' to no one in particular.

I knew what was in that storeroom: glues, timber stains, varnishes, solvents; and several gas cylinders, as well as less combustible things. The fire couldn't have started in a worse part of the factory. If even one can of those volatile liquids were to explode, it could set off a chain-reaction that would turn the factory into an inferno in a few moments.

There must be another fire-extinguisher, I thought, trying to think where I had seen them on the walls and cursing myself for not having taken more notice.

It was Keith Barnes who reached the storeroom first. Nigel shouted, 'Wait!' – and I realized that he was afraid that once the door was opened and the fire inside was given a fresh flow of air, it would flame savagely. But his warning was too late. Keith had opened the door partially, and coughed chokingly as smoke and gases hit him from inside the burning room. Then he yelled:

'Nigel! There's someone in there!'

Otto snapped, 'Don't be daft!'

But both he and Nigel ran for the storeroom. Holding the swatch of cloth half in front of his face for a shield against the heat, Nigel barged into the room shouting, 'For God's sake, Keith, get out of the building! Get out! Everyone get out!'

Flames licked out and around Nigel as he dashed into the room and Otto Klein, one arm half-raised to ward off some of the heat from his face, leaned around the doorpost and began directing the contents of his fire-extinguisher at the flames. Then as he realized I was beside him he thrust the extinguisher into my hands and went in after Nigel.

I huddled crouching at the doorway, exposing as little of myself to the fire as possible, using the same tactic Otto had used, too shocked to really be afraid.

It was probably no more than fifteen to twenty seconds from the time Nigel dived into the smoke-choked room until he and Otto stumbled out again, half-carrying, half-dragging the inert figure of a man.

'Shut that door again!' Nigel barked at me.

It was a sliding door and as I caught it to drag it across Martin stopped me, grabbed the fire-extinguisher and went on directing it its stream of chemicals at the flames.

'There's another extinguisher on the wall in the upholstery shop,' he flung at me, his face grim and intent.

I stumbled off to get it and was back with it, some part of my brain registering amazement at its weight, just as the one he was using ran out of its retardant chemicals, and he snatched the fresh one and turned it on the fire which was still spreading, the heat growing intense. I was suddenly aware that Gordon was beside me, a hose in his hands. The water from it seemed lost as it hit the flames, but I felt they were not spreading so rapidly.

Then someone pulled me backwards, and Nigel was there, shouting: 'Get out! For God's sake, leave it and get out! Let the bloody place go if it has to. Get out before those cans start blowing!'

He heaved at the door and it slid shut. But for the fact the second extinguisher had just emptied itself, I doubt if Martin would have given up. As we hurried toward the door I heard the wailing of a siren and in moments there were firemen swarming through the place with disciplined speed. One fireman with a loud-hailer was ordering people to move their cars well away from the building. I spent several numb seconds looking for mine before I remembered I hadn't brought it in this morning. It was only then that I realized I was crying – shaking with sobs as tears ran down my face. I suppose I was shocked, because to me there is always something shocking, something appallingly violent, about a burning building. But my tears were tears of rage.

From the moment Keith had shouted that there was someone in the storeroom everything else about the fire had taken on a queer aura of personal outrage. Even the fact that I had stayed to fight it – knowing the inadequacy of what we were doing – had sprung from that. At any other time, I think, I'd simply have fled the building. But the sight of that limp form that Nigel and Otto had carried out of the room had turned the fire into a personal enemy, a thing to hate, a thing to fight because it had tried to kill someone.

I looked around, my head clearing in the fresh air. A little distance from the building a group were gathered around a still figure on the grass. A fireman was holding an oxygen mask over the man's face and Nigel was kneeling on the other side of him. I couldn't see who the man was but I made myself stand back out of the way, since there was nothing I could do, and already the growing howling of a siren told that an ambulance was coming.

When it had gone again with the unconscious man I

caught Nigel's arm. 'Who is it?' I asked.

He shook his head. The skin on his face was scorched red from the fire like a very severe sunburn, and his eyes were inflamed and watering. 'I don't know.'

I stared. 'You mean he was so badly burned you couldn't recognize him?' I shuddered.

'No, no,' he said quickly. 'He's not burned – or hardly at all. Just unconscious from the smoke, I guess. I meant I don't know him.'

'But – it must have been one of our men? Someone from the factory who went in to try to put the fire out?'

'No. I think I've seen him before, but I can't recall who he is.'

He was looking past me at the factory. 'I think they've beaten it,' he said. 'I think they've beaten it!' There was a grin on his cracked lips.

I spun around, and saw he was right. There was still smoke, but much less of it, and no gleam of flame showed through the windows as the firemen poured water into the storeroom.

'They've done it! They've done it!' Martin shouted happily beside me. 'It never got out of the storeroom. There won't be any damage anywhere else except maybe a bit of smoke-staining, a bit of water.'

He grabbed me around the waist and we did some kind of impromptu dance, both laughing. Then suddenly sobering I said, 'Let's just hope that poor fellow will be all right.'

'Serve the swine right if he isn't,' Martin said harshly.

I stared. 'Martin! Why?'

He gave a short laugh. 'Well, why do you suppose he was in the building?'

'Why, I suppose he saw the smoke and – '

'That's likely! More likely he went in to *start* the fire than to put it out.'

'Arson!' I said incredulously. 'But why?'

'Most probably because someone paid him. Business can be dirty play sometimes. A factory that's been burned out is more likely to sell – and sell cheaply – than one that's still functioning.'

'Somehow,' Nigel said mildly, 'I don't see the people who want to buy us out stooping to arson. And our friend from the storeroom would have to be the greatest bungler in history if he was supposed to be an arsonist. Anyway, no doubt we'll find out in time. Meanwhile, let's get back to work. There'll be the devil of a mess to clean up.'

He was right, though the damage had been confined almost entirely to the storeroom, and there was a limit to the amount of clearing-up which could be done until the damage had been assessed for insurance, and firemen and police had checked the indications as to how the fire had started. The whole morning was taken up with sorting order from chaos and lunch-break was something people took when they could. Keith Barnes and I found ourselves with our sandwiches and thermoses of tea in a sunny corner of the factory yard at the same time.

'An interesting morning, don't you think?' he said, eyeing me intently.

'The kind of excitement I can do without,' I told him.

'Maybe. But still interesting. Think about people's reactions.'

I frowned, puzzled. 'What do you mean?'

'Just that. Everyone reacted differently. Gordon, eminently practical – wanting to save the factory and knowing it pays to get the professionals – calling the fire-brigade. Nigel quite prepared to let it burn. That's interesting for a start.'

'Nigel's prime concern was to get everyone out of the building, surely,' I pointed out. 'And surely that's the most important thing. I don't think anyone could imagine he *wanted* it to burn. He yelled at you not to open the stockroom door, because once a fire gets air it flares up.'

'Just as well I did open it,' Keith said dryly.

I shuddered. 'Yes.' I turned my head to look at him sharply. 'Why did you open it? You must have known what the fire would do once the air hit it?'

For a moment there was no sign of his usual arrogance. 'I guess for a moment I forgot. I just wanted to see inside that room. Try to see where, and maybe how, the fire had started. I really wanted to know that.'

'And?'

He shrugged. 'All I saw was somebody sprawled on the floor. Anyway, there was too much smoke. And that's part of what I mean about reactions: Gordon instantly on the phone calling the brigade; Nigel shouting at everybody to get out and let it burn; me wanting to find out why it was on fire in the first place; Martin and you and Otto using fire-extinguishers as if your lives depended on stopping the fire. You should think about it.'

And he wheeled away, back into the building, leaving me looking blankly after him. I didn't think he'd been simply philosophizing; he'd been trying to get some sort of reaction from me.

I was still puzzling over it when Nigel came out of the factory. 'Oh, there you are. I thought you'd like to know the chap in the storeroom is all right.' He grinned ruefully. 'Apparently his condition was only partly due to inhaling too much smoke: he'd drunk himself completely stoned. That's how the fire started, apparently: the old story of the half-smoked cigarette.'

'But what on earth was he *doing* in there? And how did he get in?'

'He smashed a back window. As for why – ' He paused. 'I guess it's a bit sad, really, in its way. Weird, but then you can do some very weird things when you're drunk. He used to manage the Manchester section of a department store here for years – I should have recognized him. It seemed the kind of job that lasts a lifetime. Then the store closed, and he simply couldn't get another job. He has a wife and three teenage kids. From having a good job, a comfortable life, he finally had to give in last Friday and apply for the dole. He's never been a drinking man, but his reaction was to go out and get smashed out of his mind. Some time last night, apparently, with just enough sense left to be ashamed to go home, he needed somewhere to sleep, so he did what seemed like a good idea at the time: he broke into the first building he came to. It happened to be this one, and the storeroom looked like a good place to sleep it off. And he passed out while smoking a cigarette.'

He smiled. 'So much for the arsonist theory. There won't be any charges laid against him or anything. He'll be in hospital for a few days, I should think, but I just thought you'd like to know he's all right.'

I nodded. 'Yes,' I said. 'Thank you.'

Nigel went back into the factory and I sat for a few minutes on the bench in the sun. I knew now, clearly and with absolute certainty, how I would vote at the shareholders' meeting the following night. I wondered how I could ever have had any doubts.

The meeting was held in the lounge room of Eleanor's house. I always had to keep reminding myself that it was Eleanor's house: it seemed natural to think of it as Gordon and Christine's. The children were sent off to the rumpus room, and somewhat to my surprise Eleanor came into the meeting. She came in without speaking and sat leaning back almost wearily in an easy-chair. In the week I had lived in this house I had not seen her to speak to since that first afternoon. Often at night I heard her piano, and Christine had told me that she had been a professional musician playing with a symphony orchestra before her marriage to Peter De Witt. Twice I had seen her in the garden, weeding, but as soon as I approached she had said, 'Hello,' quite pleasantly, and then walked back into the house. In response to everyone's greeting on this evening she simply nodded, said, 'Good evening,' courteously and with complete disinterest, and even when Rachael went across and kissed her, her only response was a polite smile.

Martin Weldon had been invited to attend the meeting and to present a financial report. When he had finished going through the figures he put down his sheaf of papers and looked around the assembled group.

'The company has not yet traded out of its difficulties,' he said quietly, 'but it can. I'm absolutely certain of that, and I think you would have to agree that the figures support me.'

'The contract to supply the furnishings and completely design the décor for that Melbourne restaurant was a major coup, surely,' I said. 'How did it happen that they chose Selbridges to do it?'

'That was Martin's doing,' Gordon said. 'He happened to know the fellow who was heading the syndicate which set up the restaurant by renovating and restoring what had once been virtually a mansion but had fallen into disrepair and neglect. Martin got the syndicate interested, Nigel drew up designs for the furniture and furnishings, and we got the contract. It was probably the major thing in easing us over the knife-edge of bakruptcy we were teetering on.'

'We were most fortunate to have Martin with us,' Rachael put in, smiling at him.

Marin shrugged. 'That's my job, to market the goods. But we're not normally in the market for that type of work,' he added to me. 'That happened only because it was a top-class restaurant the syndicate was setting up, and they took a calculated gamble by setting the atmosphere with luxurious furnishings. What we want most is recognition by major furniture retailers and interior-decorators. That is gradually happening and there's every reason to assume it will increase. It just isn't something that happens overnight.'

'It seems not everyone shares Martin's confidence, by the way,' Gordon said dryly. 'Mrs Robinson from the office handed in her notice today. She's been offered another job and took it.'

'The first rat leaving the sinking ship,' Martin said a shade bitterly.

'I wonder,' Nigel mused casually, 'why that's always regarded as cowardice? It sounds like common sense to me.'

'Keith Barnes said something curious to me yesterday

after the excitement of the fire had simmered down,' I said thoughtfully. 'He said it had been very interesting to see the way the people there at the time reacted in different ways. He told me I should think about it. He seemed to think it was terribly significant in some way. I don't know why.'

I was looking down, as I spoke, at the jotting-pad I'd put on the table in front of me for scribbling notes concerning points which might arise at the meeting. Something – some movement, perhaps: an involuntary gesture, a small sharp breath – made me look up swiftly, a queer prickle of alertness that was in some way akin to alarm stirring through my nerves.

Nigel was saying that a variety of reactions was pretty normal in any emergency, and there were a few minutes of general talk about the fire, and the moment had passed.

But I had the strange feeling that my casual remark had startled someone in the room, and I had been too slow to see who it was.

I was still wondering whether I had imagined it when Gordon said, 'Well, let's get back to business, shall we? We've all heard the latest possible figures on our financial position, and our accountant's prognosis. Does anyone have any questions?'

No one spoke.

'Right. I rather think that brings us to the matter of voting for or against acceptance of the offer to purchase our company. Anyone who wishes to may put his or her own case, though whether it will change anyone else's mind is probably somewhat doubtful at this stage. Within our family, I think we all know how each will vote. I asked all of you not to tell Trisha your feelings, but to let her make up her own mind. Well, no doubt she has done so.'

He paused and glanced at me with a smile, but there was a tenseness about his face-muscles and I thought suddenly: Gordon cares rather a lot; I wonder what it is he cares about – the cash in hand or the family business?

'But,' he went on, 'now, I feel, we all have the right to

influence her if we can, if she is not yet totally committed to one course. Mother, perhaps as the senior partner you might cast the first vote?'

Rachael nodded. 'Thank you, Gordon.' She looked, not at me, but at each of her children in turn. Small and slender, her grey hair perfectly groomed, she looked elegant and almost fragile in a dress of soft crimson wool. But this quietly spoken woman, I knew, had physically worked beside her husband and father-in-law in the factory when the going had been hard, and I suspected she was no fool when it came to business acumen.

'You are the third generation to own Selbridge Furniture. To me, to sell because one chooses a different occupation, a different way of life – that would be acceptable. But to sell because we merely wish to avoid defeat is to sell ourselves, and those who worked in the business before us, short. I agree with Martin that on the figures he has presented Selbridges can survive.'

She looked at me. 'I realize, Trisha, that you genuinely want to do the sensible thing, and I'm most grateful that you have taken the whole thing so seriously. Sensible simply means different things to different people, and you, most of all of us, must make the decision which seems to you the best business decision.' She smiled, her eyes twinkling. 'And none of us will think any less of you for disagreeing with us.'

She glanced back at Gordon. 'I need hardly add it, after all that, but I vote to reject the offer to purchase the company.'

Gordon formally recorded the vote. No one spoke.

Gordon looked up. 'Eleanor?'

'Accept the offer,' Eleanor said flatly.

'Do you want to give us your reasons?' her brother asked almost gently.

'I should think you'd know my reasons.'

All eyes were fixed on her, but she wasn't looking at any of us.

'I don't, really,' Gordon said. 'I knew you wanted to sell,

but not *why* you did. You needn't give any reasons, of course,' he added quickly.

Her face immobile, her voice incisive with cold bitterness, she said, 'I want to be rid of everything that ever had any connection with Julian West.'

Startled into forgetting for a moment that Martin and I were outsiders, Gordon said, 'But what about the house?'

'If Selbridges is sold you and Christine will have some money. You may buy the house if you wish. In any case I shan't put you out.'

Gordon stared at her for a moment and then with a visible effort brought himself back to the business in hand. He wrote down Eleanor's vote.

'Perhaps,' he said, 'I should ask Trisha next. But as we all know, unless one of us has changed our minds, she has the casting vote. Trisha, do you mind waiting till last?'

'No. Though I hope one of you *has* changed your mind.'

He gave me a sympathetic smile. 'I'm sorry we're putting you on the spot like this. Even now I can't tell you whether the vote has been what we expected. Well, perhaps I should say right now that I agree with Mother. I don't like accepting defeat, and I don't think we need to grasp for this offer like a drowning man. I'm in favour of rejecting the offer to purchase.'

He noted it down. The palms of my hands were tingling, though I felt a sense of relief: from the beginning I had thought neither Gordon nor Nigel would want to sell, but if one did, it would be Gordon, the practical businessman.

'Nigel?' Gordon invited.

Nigel was leaning back in his chair, hands in his trouser-pockets. 'Sell,' he said.

There was a little silence.

'Want to give reasons?' Gordon asked.

Nigel shrugged. 'Just say I want to go back to being an architect.'

The two brothers were looking at each other and I felt that each was silently questioning the other, and each knew only his own question, and neither knew the answers.

'I see,' Gordon said. 'Sorry, Trisha. Your vote.'

I felt a swift surge of unreasonable anger against Nigel.

I said, 'Until the fire yesterday I honestly didn't know what I should do. But I have known since then, and as far as I'm concerned, Selbridges is not for sale.'

A grin of pure delight spread over Martin's face. I think he wanted to cheer.

Nigel said, 'Mind telling us what the fire had to do with it?'

'I was worried all along about what would happen to some of the employees if the place was sold and the new owners simply closed it down. The older people, and Keith Barnes – where would they get jobs these days? And then there was the man you and Otto Klein got out of the storeroom: he almost died and almost burned the factory down because he got blind drunk to forget what it was like to be unemployed. I'm sure we owe something to the people who have worked here before us. But I think we owe even more to those who work here now. It's quite possible business *won't* improve and the company will go down the sink anyway, and it will be obvious I have made a wrong decision. If that happens I'll be very sorry. But there's a fair chance Selbridges will survive and prosper, and I think we should take that chance.'

I stopped. 'Sorry. I didn't mean to make a speech. And – look, I've worked in an office all my working life. If you'll have me, I'll take over Mrs Robinson's job; and until the company is on its feet I'll settle for less than her wages.'

'I'm sure we'd all be delighted to have you,' Gordon said warmly.

'Thank you,' I said. 'And now I feel there may be things you want to dicuss as a family, so if you'll excuse me I've some letters to write.'

There were murmured goodnights and Nigel got up to open the door for me. He smiled down at me a little ruefully – almost sadly. 'I'm proud you did what you did, Trisha.

But I rather wish you were going back to Melbourne.'

The enigma of the remark didn't really register until I was in the hall. I turned quickly to look at him, but he had gone back into the living-room and closed the door.

Six

In the weeks that followed I moved into a small flat in town because I felt I couldn't impose on Gordon and Christine's hospitality, and in any case I preferred to be independent, and so I settled down to work in the office of Selbridge Furniture.

Most weekends I went riding with Martin, loving it and gradually becoming more at home in a saddle. I couldn't share Martin's enthusiasm for his other sports, which were deep-sea fishing and surf-board riding. He knew an elderly man who owned a small cabin cruiser – at least, it looked small to me: much too small to face the hazards of the open ocean. The owner now rarely used the boat but was happy to hire it out. Martin was hugely amused by my reluctance to join him on fishing expeditions.

'The weather's perfect and I'm only going out to the Six-Mile Reef – not on a trans-Pacific epic,' he'd say. 'What can go wrong?'

'That Six-Mile Reef sound suspiciously as if it might be at least five-and-three-quarter miles too far from shore,' I told him. 'Have fun and leave me to my cowardice.'

I also became firm friends with Rhelma Barnes, who occasionally came riding with Martin and me, and sometimes when Martin was out fishing she and I went riding on Martin's horses, which he cheerfully offered for our use whenever we wished. Rhelma was an excellent horsewoman and I felt she had greatly missed riding, which she had not done for a long time because she had no horse.

And since she worked part-time she hadn't much opportunity for relaxation. In spite of his fierce determination to be as independent as possible, Keith's handicap must have entailed extra work for Rhelma in caring for him. He seemed pleased for her to go out with me, and sometimes his manner towards me almost bordered on civility.

Business at the factory certainly didn't boom, but it didn't decrease either. I was busy and I was as happy as I had ever been in my life. There was nothing to suggest that all might not be well in my world.

Martin phoned one Saturday morning to ask if I would drive him down to the Marina to pick up the boat for one of his fishing expeditions, and then collect him again in the evening and drive him home.

'Sorry to trouble you, Trisha, but I've already arranged to hire the boat and now my stupid car decides to pack it in on a weekend – some problem with rear brakes seizing.'

'Oh, I don't mind being a taxi-driver,' I told him cheerfully. 'It's only when it comes to being a deckhand that I draw the line.'

When I went to his house next morning to pick him up he came out looking, as I told him, just simply too dashing in an elderly and floppy cloth hat, raggy shorts, and sneakers that smelled of fish before he even set out, and hung about with all kinds of gear.

'I can't help wondering,' I commented, 'whether a few fish are worth all the trouble. You look as if you're setting out on a trans-Tasman crossing at the very least.'

He grinned. 'Certain gear one must have. Certain more gear is a good idea. And if you think it's just the fish, you should come out one day and find out what the sport is like. Incidentally, I haven't got all the necessary equipment yet. I left my first-aid kit securely locked away in my car, which I now realize is locked away in Spencer's Garage ready for them to work on tomorrow. Would you drop by the factory and I'll nick the box from there.'

I looked at him. 'So you do take the sea seriously.'

'In spite of laughing at you for being afraid of it? Only a fool doesn't take the sea seriously or fails to understand risks. That doesn't mean you should run away from them.'

'Sometimes,' I said slowly, 'I think I understand you very well. And sometimes I don't think I understand you at all.'

He stood for a moment looking at me, his eyes gentle. He bent and kissed me lightly. 'Just love me anyway.'

I delivered him to the Marina with a promise to return for him at five. 'Take care,' I said.

He held up the first-aid box we had picked up from the factory. It was the size of a small suitcase and comprehensively equipped. 'Never fear. With this I'm practically ready to handle major surgery.'

'Oh, just a couple of small amputations will do,' I assured him.

' "Oh, woman, when pain and anguish wring the brow, a ministering angel, thou",' he quoted cheerfully. 'For being a good girl I'll buy you a drink at the club when I get back. We might even have an expensive dinner.'

'With you dressed like that? And smelling worse? They'd never let you in the door.'

'Somewhere in all this equipment I have something else to wear. When you see me again I shall be a changed man.'

He tossed me a broad wink and clambered aboard the neat little red-and-white cruiser, while I drove away wondering what was the magic spell that possessed fishermen and filled them with such exuberance at the thought of spending hours on a rolling boat getting either frozen or sunburned in the search for those elusive and rather beautiful creatures, the sight of which on the end of a nylon line occasions such delight. And I began to wonder also whether Martin and I were becoming rather more than the proverbial good friends.

He was as good as his word, and when I reached the Marina about five he had just finished mooring the boat and was now neat and spruce in slacks and blazer.

'Good day?' I asked as we stowed his belongings in the boot of my car.

'Look at that,' he said for answer, opening up his portable ice-box to show me his catch. 'Schnapper. Red Emperor. Coral trout.'

'And two cans of beer untouched. You must have been busy. Or seasick.'

He laughed. 'Never go to sea unless fully prepared for emergencies. I told you that this morning.'

The club bar was just pleasantly busy, and Martin fell easily into conversation with a stocky little man with brightly shrewd eyes behind rimless glasses who, when Martin introduced me and himself, said his name was John Clinton and added that he was up from Melbourne on holiday.

I looked at him with quick interest. 'John Clinton Interiors?' I asked, the question surprised out of me without my really intending to ask it.

He nodded, eyeing me questioningly.

'Sorry,' I said quickly. 'I didn't mean to sound prying. It's just that – well, Martin and I are involved in the furniture manufacturing business, and so I was interested to hear your name.'

He said, 'What sort of furniture do you make?' in a tone which suggested it must be pretty uninteresting junk.

With a flicker of annoyance I said, 'Perhaps you know the Falkner Mansions Restaurant. Selbridges did the furnishing.'

His expression changed slightly, and I felt with a touch of triumph that he was considerably surprised and no longer so contemptuous. Several martinis later he had declared he would be most interested to see what Selbridge Furniture had to offer and would visit the factory next day.

As Martin and I left I remarked on the good fortune of the chance meeting. 'John Clinton Interiors is a big name in quality furniture and furnishings in Melbourne,' I said. 'Even I know of them. If he does turn up at the factory tomorrow and is suitably impressed it could be an important foot in the marketing door.'

There was a mischievous twinkle in Martin's eyes. 'I know about John Clinton Interiors, too, and it wasn't really a chance meeting. I knew he was holidaying here, and that he's a boating man, so there was a good chance he'd be around the club sometime. I've been haunting the place for a fortnight. I had Albert in the bar alerted to point him out to me.'

'Oh-ho! So the object of the exercise wasn't really to buy me a much-deserved drink?'

He chuckled. 'Now don't tell me you mind mixing a little business with pleasure. You did your sales pitch very well. I didn't need to say anything.'

'Mmm. I got a bit prickly when I could positively hear him dismissing Selbridge Furniture as something cheap and nasty. I couldn't resist tossing in the bit about Falkner Mansions. Did you really go to all that trouble just to make a possible business contact? You really care about Selbridge Furniture, don't you?'

I flung a quick sideways glance at him. His eyes were on the black ribbon of bitumen unrolling in the car's headlights, and there was something intent – more, oddly *intense* – about his profile.

'It's my job,' he said lightly enough. 'I just like to succeed at the things I take on, that's all.'

We were coming into the town. 'I think I like that kind of attitude,' I said. 'Aunt Agnes was like that.'

'I'm glad she'd have approved of me,' he said. 'Where are we going?' he added as I turned out of the main street.

'Just to drop the first-aid kit back at the factory.'

'Oh, Lord, I'm glad you remembered. Gordon would have my head if I'd nicked his precious gear and failed to return it.'

We took the box into the factory and when we got back into the car I said musingly, 'I wonder if Mr Clinton will come tomorrow?'

'He'll come,' Martin said confidently. 'It wasn't just the martinis. He'll come.'

I was still wondering whether John Clinton would turn up at the factory when I arrived for work on the Monday morning, and probably that was why I managed to let the car door swing closed again before I got out, catching my right hand against the frame and cutting two fingers. The injury wasn't much, though it was quite painful and bleeding messily, so as I was the first to arrive at the factory and there was no one else about, I had to fumble left-handedly in my handbag for my keys and let myself into the building, heading for the office and some dressings for my wounds. I felt it wasn't a very auspicious start to the day.

I was struggling somewhat unsuccessfully with a bandage when Martin came in. 'Hello,' he said. 'What've you done to your hand?'

'Left it in the car when I closed up,' I said ruefully. 'I don't think it was a good idea.'

'Here,' he said concernedly. 'Let me do that. Are you sure it's all right? No fractures? What about seeing a doctor?'

I shook my head. 'It's nothing really – just messy and rather sore. I'm quite glad, though, that we didn't leave the first-aid box on the boat last night.'

'Yes.' He was bandaging carefully. 'It just proves you should never take these things away from where they belong. Next time I take the boat out I'll make jolly sure I have my own or none at all. I'd have felt pretty rotten if this had happened and there'd been nothing here to treat you with. How does that feel?'

'That's fine.'

'You mean hurting like hell.'

'Not really. Though I suppose if I'd had any sense I'd have put some of that antiseptic powder on it before it was bandaged, wouldn't I?'

'I guess it would have been a good idea. Well, we can unbandage it.' He picked up the packet. 'No, apparently not

– it's away past the expiry date marked on it. I'll throw it out. Sometimes things like that can do more harm than good if they're old. But if you have any doubts about the way that hand feels by lunchtime, you really must see a doctor.'

'You sound like a television advertisement for aspirin. Anyway, it was my own stupid fault. I was thinking of your Mr Clinton and wondering if he really might turn up. When I did this I concluded it was a bad omen.'

'Of course he'll turn up,' Martin said. 'After I plied him with grog and you charmed him, how could he fail?'

He went out and I saw Keith Barnes at the doorway, watching. Sometimes I found there was something unnerving about Keith. He always seemed to be *watching* people. Not crudely, not even out of idle curiosity. That was what made it unnerving. There seemed to be something important about it.

Now, as I looked up and saw him, there was an extraordinary expression in his face, but at once it changed and became guarded and cynical again.

'Did you go out deep-sea fishing with Martin yesterday?' he asked civilly enough.

'No, thank you!' I said with feeling. 'I get seasick and anyway I hate fishing.'

'You don't recognize good sport when you see it,' Keith retorted, and wheeled away, and I settled down to work as best I could with one hand bandaged and rather more painful than I wanted to admit, so cross was I with my own clumsiness.

But the bad start to the day was cancelled out later in the morning when John Clinton did indeed arrive at the factory. He not only came, he stayed a considerable time, and when he went he left behind a considerable and valuable order and a general air of delighted optimism throughout the factory. To have one foot in the door of John Clinton Interiors was a reason for some optimism. Even Keith Barnes seemed in good humour.

Certainly there didn't seem to be in anyone's mind the faintest premonition of tragedy.

The weeks had run into months and the winter of my arrival had run into summer, with fairly frequent afternoon thunderstorms, and on the Friday afternoon following John Clinton's visit there was a storm with very heavy rain. Martin and I were to go riding on the Saturday morning, and when I drove up to his stables he was just saddling our horses – Mindy, his favourite mare, and the dapple-grey gelding called Condor whose good manners made my inexperience less obvious.

'I thought we might ride up the range to the National Park and have a look at the falls,' Martin suggested. 'It's very pretty up there and the falls will be quite spectacular with the run-off water from last night's storm. There's a nice little restaurant near there where we can have lunch.'

It was a delightful ride. The day was made of blue sky and gold sun tempered by a breeze from the sea some fifteen or twenty kilometres to the east, and Martin knew a short cut from his place to the top of the range and had permission to ride across someone's farm pasture. Yesterday's storm had washed the air sparkling clean and the sweeping views were clear, and the birds seemed to sing especially joyously. Martin and I chatted happily or could ride in silence just as contentedly, looking at the world around us.

The falls were indeed swollen by the night rain, and from the pool just back from the edge of the cliff – which Martin said was normally a fairly popular swimming-pool but which was today decidedly unsafe because of the volume of rushing water – the little creek leapt out to crash in foaming white among the rocks far below. We tethered the horses and walked down the path through the moist greenness of virgin rain forest to get a better view of the falls from below.

'Normally,' Martin explained, 'It's only a little stream, and though the falls are high they're usually pretty, rather than spectacular. There's quite a volume of water coming over there today, though.'

We stood watching for a while, caught by that special mesmeric spell of tumbling water. A whip-bird swung his verbal stock-whip almost beside us, unafraid. But high overhead a pair of wedge-tailed eagles soared in effortless circles on their great wings, watching for prey in the tree-tops below – a reminder that the peace and tranquillity of nature is an illusion, and that even in these idyllic surroundings life for the natural inhabitants is an endless struggle which only the fit and the lucky survive.

We walked back to the top of the falls, the track a bit muddy and inclined to be slippery.

'Just watch your footing on this bit,' Martin said – and as he spoke one foot slipped from under him and he landed on hands and knees. 'Says he, demonstrating,' he added with a grin as he scrambled up. He looked ruefully at the knees of his jeans. 'Rather spoils my general debonair look, just when I was taking you to lunch.'

'Oh, you can sponge the worst of it out in the creek when we get to the top,' I told him cheerfully. 'You don't get out of taking me to lunch that easily.'

There weren't many people about – possibly most people felt that after the storm the rain-soaked ground wasn't ideal for either picnicking or walking. While Martin was washing the mud from his hands and brushing it off his jeans at the edge of the pool above the falls, I went to untie the horses.

As I turned to lead them back to where Martin was, I saw the edge of the bank where he was standing crumble. He overbalanced and fell into the pool.

I screamed, 'Martin!' – and watched in helpless horror as he fought to swim back to the bank. The current had swept him several metres out from the bank and, desperately as he tried to swim against it, it pulled him relentlessly toward the cliff edge where the water leapt dizzily down to the rocks far below.

Several people, seeing what was happening, ran futilely towards the pool. I stood where I was, anchored like someone trapped by the cruel fetters of an electric current.

Every detail of what I was seeing was so imprinted on my awareness that it was like seeing a film run in slow motion. The whole thing could have only a few seconds, yet it seemed quite a long time.

Lifting himself as high in the water as he could, Martin shouted, 'Mindy! Mindy!'

The mare's head came up, ears pricked, and she bounded forward as I dropped the reins.

'Go, Mindy, go,' I whispered, and began to run to the pool.

Martin was thrashing at the water now with all his strength, trying to edge toward the bank, trying to beat the slow certainty with which the stream dragged him to death. But it was too strong.

With neither haste nor hesitation, as if it were just another of their hide-and-seek games, the big mare slid into the pool and in a second was beside Martin. He locked his fingers on to the stirrup-leather and shouted, 'Out, girl! Up!'

She seemed to fully understand the danger, for she instantly stuck out, snorting, for the bank. For a moment she seemed unable to make any headway, and then somehow she was scrambling out, dragging Martin with her.

He let go of the stirrup-leather and sprawled for a moment face down on the grass while Mindy shook herself vigorously and stood watching curiously while everyone gathered around Martin asking if he was all right. I heard one man say, 'My God, that horse deserves a medal. That was the quickest thing I ever saw.'

Quickest. I realized it must have been, but to me it seemed an age – the longest few seconds I had ever spent.

Martin got to his feet. His chest was still heaving as he gulped air, his sodden hair was plastered to his scalp and his clothes still ran rivulets of creek water. I thought I had never seen anyone look so wonderful.

He said, 'I'm fine. Thanks, everyone.'

Then I flung myself into his arms, shuddering. I think I was sobbing. Certainly I was incapable of speech. I clung to him fiercely, feeling the strength and warmth of his body through his saturated clothes as he wrapped his arms tightly around me. Perhaps he needed the feel of me in his arms as a confirmation of life as much as I needed the reassurance that he really was alive and safe.

Presently he kissed me and held me away a little, smiling down at me.

'Now you're nearly as wet as I am,' he said, just the tiniest hint of unsteadiness in his voice. He laid one hand gently against my cheek. 'Hey, come on! Don't look like that. It didn't happen.'

One arm still around me, he fondled Mindy's mane and ears, patting her neck. 'Good girl,' he said over and over. 'Good girl.'

I couldn't stop shivering, even when we rode out of the rain-forest park into the bright summer sun. It was only at the restaurant – where, alerted by other people who had been at the falls, they made rather a fuss of us and loaned Martin dry clothes – that a brandy finally warmed through my shock.

During our lunch we probably talked and laughed a little too much from the sheer joy of being alive. On the ride home we were probably a little too quiet for the same reason. I couldn't know what he was thinking, but I knew now, whatever doubts I may have had about it before, that I had fallen in love with Martin Weldon.

Seven

It was on the following Wednesday evening just as I was about to go to bed, somewhere between ten and ten-thirty, that Nigel phoned me at my flat.

'Trish, I'm sorry to do this to you,' he said quietly, 'but something terrible has happened. Could you come around to the Barnes's house? Rhelma needs a friend right now, and I guess you're the closest friend she has. Keith is dead.'

'Keith!' I gripped the phone as if for support. The arrogant, ill-mannered, ill-tempered Keith who somehow in spite of being confined to a wheelchair had always radiated sheer, forceful, storming life. Keith dead?

'But – what? How?'

'I'll meet you outside the house. Can you come?'

'Yes. Yes, of course. Five minutes.'

As I approached the Barnes's neat, unpretentious house in a quiet but pleasantly-situated street I could see the lights were on in every room and a little group of people outside were wandering about in aimless curiosity. Rhelma's car was parked in the street, prevented from entering the driveway because a police car was standing in the entrance, and another was parked in the street. Nigel's car was parked in front of the house and I pulled my car in behind Rhelma's as Nigel came hurrying out, watched by a uniformed policeman who stood by the front door.

I caught Nigel's arm. 'He had an accident? Where's Rhelma?'

'She's inside. Wait, Trish.' He put a hand on my shoulder

as I started towards the house. 'It wasn't an accident.'

I swung around to stare at him in the light from the house and a distant street-light.

He still had that unruffled air, but there was tension in the set of his jaw and his eyes were troubled.

'But – it couldn't have been a heart attack or something like that, or the police wouldn't be here. So what – ' I stopped. 'Nigel, are you saying he killed himself? *Keith?*'

He shook his head. 'No, Trish. He was murdered.'

I'm not sure how many seconds it might have taken for me to really understand what he had said. I seemed to stare open-mouthed at him for a long time.

'I'm sorry,' he said. 'I just don't know any way of saying that without it sounding brutal. God knows, I tried when I had to tell Rhelma.'

I picked up some of my scattered wits. 'Rhelma wasn't here? Or didn't it happen here? Nigel – who?'

'I don't think it's going to be all that easy to find out who. But then of course I'm not a policeman. He was killed in the living-room while Rhelma was out visiting friends. Do you think you can come in? She's pretty shocked. She wouldn't let me call a doctor, but I think right now seeing a friend would help.'

'Yes, of course,' I said mechanically, and we went into the house, Nigel pausing a moment to explain to the police officer at the door who I was. He nodded and stepped aside for us to go in.

There were two men in business suits in the living-room, and a policewoman in uniform, but they only dimly registered on the edge of my awareness. Rhelma was sitting on the sofa of the combined lounge and dining-room, looking somehow shrunken, her face deathly pale against the auburn of her hair, her eyes – usually twinkling with good humour and a readiness to laugh – were dark and staring. One of the men was speaking to her when we walked in and he paused and turned to look at us.

Rhelma looked up at me and in a voice utterly devoid of

life said, 'He's dead.'

I was glad I hadn't had any time to think about what I should do, or say to her. Without any conscious thought at all I crossed the room to sit beside her and put my arms around her. She put her face against my shoulder and began to cry wordlessly. I held her tightly without speaking for perhaps two or three minutes until presently her sobs ceased.

Pulling herself together she said, 'Oh, Trish, I'm so glad you came. Sorry for going to pieces.'

'Don't be,' I said.

'I've got to keep my head clear somehow, for Keith's sake,' she said. 'He'd have hated for me to act the little muddled woman. More than that, I have to be able to think. Because there might be something, somewhere, that I can remember that might give some clue as to who did this.'

She looked squarely at me, the blue-grey eyes still dark with shock but for a moment they glittered with hard anger. 'Because I want whoever killed him caught.'

As she said the words all the gentleness of her nature was swept away as the deep, primitive instinct to protect one's own rose over everything, except that protection was too late, and the good-natured little hairdresser might have been a Boadicea – a warrior queen bent on vengeance.

I think even the police felt the raw and powerful emotion which seemed momentarily to fill the room. No one moved for several seconds, and then the older man cleared his throat.

'I'm sorry to plague you, Mrs Barnes, but do you feel able to answer a few more questions?'

'Yes,' she said steadily.

'You say you were visiting friends.' He checked his notebook. 'Armitages. What time did you get there?'

'About seven forty-five, I think. I left about nine-thirty.'

'What was your husband doing when you left?'

'Watching television.'

'Where was he sitting?'

'In his wheelchair, just about there.' She indicated.

I realized for the first time, with an almost physical sense of shock, that his wheelchair was standing in the room beside the dining-table, and a sheet had been spread over the floor beside and in front of it, whether to cover bloodstains or preserve the area for forensic examination – or both – I had no idea; but it was a stark reminder that a few minutes ago a man's body had lain there.

'His chair was not by the table where it is now?'

'No.'

'There's a ball-point pen on the table. Was it usually there?'

She glanced at it. 'I couldn't be sure it's ours – it's a very common type. There wouldn't usually be a pen on that table, but then it wouldn't be so very unusual, either.'

'Had your husband mentioned he was expecting anyone to call?'

'No.'

'Yet Mr Selbridge says he telephoned him, rather late, and asked him to come around.'

She shook her head. 'He didn't mention wanting to see Nigel.'

'Did he often invite friends to the house if you were out? Did he get lonely?'

'I very rarely went out at night without him. I don't recall him ever asking anyone to come.'

'What had his manner been lately? Did he seem worried, excited – anything unusual?'

Rhelma seemed to think for a moment, and then said: 'No, I don't think so.'

'Would your front door normally be locked?'

'Not until we were going to bed.'

The policeman looked at her intently. 'So anyone could have walked in off the street?'

'I suppose so, yes. It's a very quiet neighbourhood. We just never thought about things like locking doors while we were still moving about.'

'Would your husband have been carrying much money? Or did you have money in the house?'

'No. Nothing of consequence.'

'Would you go with Constable Jenkins and check whether anything is missing – jewellery, watches, portable radio, binoculars, electrical goods – anything?'

Rhelma stood up mechanically and went out with the policewoman. Vaguely I had registered the sound of a car stopping outside, and now a man came in with a bag rather like a doctor's bag. The senior detective looked at him enquiringly and he shook his head. 'Nothing,' he said. He carefully rolled the sheet back from the floor, set up a bright light on a tripod and on hands and knees began meticulously studying the carpet. Then he carefully began dusting the wheelchair with powder.

The man who had been doing all the questioning turned to me. He was a thin, neat man with disconcertingly bright blue eyes.

'You're Miss Kent, of course,' he said. 'I'm Detective Sergeant Cunningham.' He nodded at the younger man, a big sandy-haired fellow who carried just a shade too much weight. 'Detective Wilkes.'

We exchanged nods.

'You and Mrs Barnes are close friends?'

'We haven't known each other very long – about four or five months. But we have become good friends, yes.'

'Would you say she and her husband were happy?'

'Yes, I would.'

'He had the reputation of being – rather difficult.'

I suppose I looked surprised, and he smiled. 'The advantages of being a detective in a small town,' he said. 'You tend to pick up background information on people.'

The initial numbness of shock at what had happened was beginning to clear from my brain. 'Then you should also know that Keith was never rude to Rhelma and she adored him,' I said.

'Did you like Keith Barnes, Miss Kent?'

I hesitated because it seemed cruel to say it. 'Not really,' I said.

'Because he was consistently ill-mannered?'

'Yes. I tried to like him, but he made it very difficult.'

'Yet you're sure he and his wife were happy?'

'Yes. Or at least – I mean happy with each other. I suppose a man like Keith could never be really happy confined to a wheelchair.'

'Quite.'

I frowned. 'I don't think I see what you're getting at, Sergeant. Is there a possibility Keith committed suicide?'

'No.'

'You're sure?'

His intent eyes were steady on mine. 'It's very difficult to crush the back of your own skull with an axe and then wipe it clean of fingerprints before dropping it on the floor.'

He said it with casual, deliberate bluntness, watching me.

My eyes flicked instinctively to the wheelchair and I felt myself almost flinch. 'Oh,' I said flatly. Then something registered. 'Axe?' I demanded sharply.

'The New Guinean native war-axe which I believe hung on the wall.'

I glanced at once to the spot on the wall where the skilfully-made artefact had hung, its brackets now empty. I knew he had noted that I knew exactly where the axe had been, and I felt anger begin to rise in me. I was being questioned as if I were a suspect.

It was only then that I realized that we were all suspects – everyone who had known Keith Barnes. And I also realized for the first time that the sergeant's questions had been directed not so much at myself as to learn what I knew of Rhelma's relationship with her husband.

Startled into foolish words, I said, 'You can't think *Rhelma* killed him?'

He said evenly, 'I haven't any preconceived ideas, Miss Kent. We merely want to arrive at the truth. To do that, we may need to sift through a great deal of information – most

A Toast to Cousin Julian   83

of which no doubt will be quite irrelevant.'

'But you said Rhelma was visiting friends: surely that's proof she wasn't even here?'

'Mrs Barnes said she was visiting friends,' he said mildly. 'We will, of course, check all that sort of thing. The doctor's preliminary examination of the body placed the time of death within the time-range which would allow for it to have occurred as early as seven to seven-thirty – before Mrs. Barnes says she left the house. Or as late as eight-thirty, when Mr Selbridge says he arrived at the house.'

I jerked my head around to look at Nigel. He was watching the detective sergeant impassively, but I knew he was perfectly aware of the deliberate implications of Sergeant Cunningham's remark. The sergeant, I reflected with somewhat reluctant admiration, was skilled enough at interrogation. He was happy to probe, watching for any reaction to suggest he had touched a raw nerve.

In the kitchen I could hear the sound of voices and the rattle of cups, muffled by the closed door, as the police-woman made Rhelma tea or coffee, and I realized that part of her job was to keep Rhelma away while the sergeant questioned Nigel and me.

He turned to Nigel. 'About what time did you say it was when Mr Barnes telephoned you, Mr Selbridge?'

'Just about eight o'clock.'

'And you came immediately?'

'Not immediately. I hadn't quite finished my dinner. I finished that and washed up. I live alone,' he added.

'So you didn't feel there was any real urgency about Mr Barnes's request that you come to see him?'

'Not really.'

'But surely it was unusual for one of your company's employees to phone at eight o'clock and request you to visit him?'

'Yes.'

'Did Mr Barnes indicate there was any urgency?'

Nigel hesitated. 'It depends what you mean by urgency. I

can be wise now and feel I should have come at once. But
there was certainly nothing in what he said, nor in the
manner he said it, to suggest he was in any kind of danger.
He did insist, when I asked if it couldn't wait till morning
and we could talk about it at work, that he wanted to see me
tonight and in private. I told him I'd be around in about
half an hour. He certainly seemed satisfied with that.'

'There was no mention of any other person?'

'No. Unless you count the fact that he said Rhelma had
gone out.'

'When you arrived, what did you do?'

'Rang the front doorbell. There was no sound from the
house, so after waiting a couple of minutes or so in case
Keith was on the phone or in the toilet or something, I rang
the bell again. Then I knocked a couple of times, walked
around to the back of the house and knocked again, and
called. I tried the back door but it was locked, so I came
back to the front door and tried that. It opened, and I came
in.'

'Why?'

Nigel raised an eyebrow. 'A man had just telephoned me
to come and see him on what presumably he considered an
important matter. I hardly thought he'd then decided to go
out. In fact, I'd seen his car in the carport. I wondered if
he'd been taken ill, or met with some kind of accident.'

The man with the fingerprint and various other
equipment was still working his way around the room.

'And what exactly did you see when you came in?' the
sergeant asked.

'Exactly what *you* saw when you came in,' Nigel answered.
'I didn't move anything. Keith was lying huddled on the
floor beside his wheelchair. I went to him, saw the head
injury and routinely knelt down and felt for his pulse, even
though I knew he must be dead. Then I went to the
telephone and called the police. I didn't touch anything else.
I didn't shift the position of the body.'

'The lights in the house were on?'

'The lights in here, the kitchen light – they were on.'

'On your way here, did you see anyone who might have come from this house?'

'I met vehicles, of course. I can't honestly recall whether I met any in this street. I don't think I met any pedestrians in this street. Certainly no one acting suspiciously.'

'After you found the body, did it strike you as strange that the lights in the house were on?'

Nigel looked faintly surprised. 'I didn't really think about it.'

'Someone walks into the house, kills a man, leaves the body on the floor with the weapon beside it, and walks out – leaving the lights on. That would greatly increase the likelihood of being seen and perhaps recognized. Surely it would have been better to turn the lights out?'

I saw Nigel's jaw tighten. 'The lights which were on when you arrived were on when *I* arrived. I neither turned any on nor any off. Why the murderer left them on is something you should ask him. Maybe he thought turning them off so early in the night would look unusual – something the neighbours might notice, and so more or less fix the time of the murder. That might have been important to whoever did it because he didn't have an alibi for that time. I don't know. As I said, ask him.'

'Or her. Oh, I shall. Mr Selbridge, you appear to have a bloodstain on the right knee of your trousers.'

Nigel glanced at a small brown mark on beige slacks. 'I knelt down beside the body.' He put a hand in his pocket and took out a stained handkerchief. 'I also got some blood on my hand when I felt Keith's wrist for a pulse, because his hands were almost under his face, as you saw, and there was some blood. I wiped my hand. You may have the handkerchief. Whether you believe I used it to wipe my hand or to wipe fingerprints from the axe is up to you. You may also,' he added dryly, 'have my trousers for examination under a microscope or whatever you do, but I would prefer you collected them later.'

There was no flicker of expression on the sergeant's face. 'I don't think that will be necessary. We will keep the handkerchief, thank you.'

His bright eyes turned to me. 'Do you live alone, Miss Kent?'

'Yes.'

'Where were you earlier this evening – before Mr Selbridge phoned and asked you to come here?'

'In my flat. I haven't any witnesses to that.'

I had a queer, unreal feeling. It just wasn't possible that I could be a murder suspect, however much the police might regard me as an outside chance.

'We have to ask all these questions, Miss Kent,' the younger man who was taking notes said unexpectedly, as if he knew what I was thinking. 'It's all part of the routine.'

The policewoman opened the door from the kitchen. 'Coffee, Sergeant?'

'Thanks. Make it for everyone, would you?'

He turned back to Nigel. 'When Mr Barnes telephoned you, what exactly did he say? The exact words, or as near as you can recall them?'

Nigel frowned in thought for a moment. 'I think he said: "Nigel, can you come around? There's something I want to talk about." I said couldn't it wait till morning and he said, "It's not the kind of thing I want to talk about at work, or even in front of Rhelma. She's gone out. Can you come? It's important." So I said I'd be around in about half an hour. He just said, "Good," and hung up.'

'He didn't say whethe or not it was something connected with Selbridge Furniture?'

'No. I admit I did wonder if he'd found out something wrong about one of the employees there. He's – he was – a *nosey* kind of fellow, yet not in a petty or obnoxious way. He just seemed to like to know everything he could about people.'

For the first time there was a flicker of a smile in Sergeant Cunningham's face. 'He'd have made a good policeman.

What was his manner when he phoned you? Did he seem agitated? Worried?'

Nigel hesitated. 'Not agitated, and not exactly worried. But serious – almost grim.'

'You got the impression that something was wrong? That he was concerned about something?'

'Concerned, yes.'

'Yet you didn't bother to come around for another half-hour.'

'I didn't get the impression it was urgent, and when I said I'd be about half an hour he seemed quite satisfied.' Nigel sounded faintly irritated at having to repeat it.

'And you did arrive half an hour later?'

'About that. I didn't look at the time.'

'And you also live alone, Mr Selbridge?'

'Yes. And like Miss Kent I have no one to confirm that I was at home in the earlier part of the evening, or that I received any phone call,' he said calmly.

The policewoman opened the kitchen door again. 'Ready for coffee, Sergeant?'

'Thank you, yes.'

The man who had been doing what I presumed were fingerprint checks had taken his equipment and departed.

Rhelma came out with Constable Jenkins, who set a tray of mugs of coffee on a side table and at a word from the sergeant took one out to the officer at the door. In spite of the warm night Rhelma had put on a jacket, but when she sat beside me on the sofa she was still shivering.

'Mrs Barnes,' Sergeant Cunningham said quietly, 'would you like me to call a doctor?'

She shook her head. 'I'm all right, thank you. Really.'

'We'll leave you in peace very soon now,' he assured her. 'We'll need to get a statement from you signed, but that can wait till morning. Is there anyone at all you'd like me to phone – friends, relatives? I shouldn't like to think you stayed alone tonight. You've had a severe shock.'

'Come around to my flat,' I suggested.

She shook her head again. 'I'd rather stay, thank you. I have to, sometime. It might as well be now. But if you could stay here, Trish – '

'Of course,' I said.

'Mrs Barnes, was there anything missing, anything disturbed?'

'No, nothing that I could see.'

He nodded as if that was what he'd expected. Coffee finished, he stood up.

'I'll leave a man outside the house all night if you wish, Mrs Barnes. And certainly I'll arrange for a patrol car to come by frequently.'

'There's no need, Sergeant,' Rhelma said steadily. 'No one would want to harm me.'

He looked at her with that bright-eyed interest. 'Do you know why someone wanted to harm your husband?'

'If I did, I would tell you. I promise you that. But I assume he was killed to prevent him from telling Nigel whatever it was he intended to tell him. I have no idea what that was, nor who or what it concerned. I wish I did.'

When at last the police had all gone, Rhelma said, 'The bed in the spare room's made up, Trisha. Will you excuse me? Thank you for staying.'

She turned and went out of the room. Nigel looked at me with a little frown. 'Do you think she's all right?'

'I think so. As all right as she can be. Wondering how she can get through the next twenty-four hours, let alone the rest of her life, I should think. She loved him. Very much.'

'Do you think she really has no idea why he was killed?'

I looked at him sharply. 'Why should she have any idea?'

'I don't know,' he said slowly. 'But – I just wondered.' He shrugged. 'Will you feel nervous, staying here?'

'I don't think so. Anyway, the patrol car will be around, keeping an eye on the place.'

'Yes, of course. But I'll doss down on the sofa if you like.'

'Don't be silly, you'd be horribly uncomfortable. And whoever killed Keith didn't come here with mass murder in mind. When he came here, he didn't even intend to kill Keith.'

Nigel's eyes narrowed. 'How the devil do you know that?'

'Well, if you intend to kill someone, surely you go prepared. You take a weapon – you don't just rely on the chance that there'll be a suitable one on hand.'

Nigel rubbed his chin, and a faint twinkle of sardonic amusement touched his eyes. 'Good thinking. I wonder if that will occur to the good sergeant?'

'I rather suspect,' 'that there's very little that *doesn't* occur to the good sergeant. If I were a criminal I don't think I'd like him on my trail.'

'You're probably right.' He paused for a moment. 'So I wonder if Keith phoned someone else to come – someone he knew something about – and confronted him with whatever the information was. But then why phone me as well?'

'If it comes to that, if you have damning evidence, or even very grave suspicions of someone, do you *tell* them?'

'Not unless you're planning blackmail, and I can't see Keith in a blackmailer's role.'

'No, neither can I. So perhaps he didn't realize how serious the whole thing was – whatever it was. Or he knew of something criminal but didn't know to whom the evidence pointed – maybe never guessed for a moment the person he was talking to was the guilty party.'

I rubbed a hand over my eyes. 'Oh, I don't know. It's all horrible. We sit here talking about it as if it's all a theory. But it isn't. A man we knew – worked with – is dead.'

Nigel touched my shoulder gently, said goodnight and left.

I locked the doors and checked the window-catches. And suddenly I knew that, midnight or not, I wanted to talk to Martin. I dialled his number and was surprised when he answered at once.

'Oh, Martin, it's Trisha. I thought I'd be waking you up. I had to talk to you. Something horrible has happened: Keith Barnes is dead.'

'Yes,' he said soberly. 'I know. I have two detectives here right now. Are you all right, Trisha? How's Rhelma?'

'She's gone to bed. I doubt if she'll sleep. She's horribly shocked, naturally. I'm staying with her for the night.'

'Wouldn't it have been better to take her to your place?' There was an edge of anxiety in his tone.

'She didn't want to go. And we'll be perfectly safe. The police will keep an eye on the place, and anyway whoever it was will never come back.'

'No, of course not. But – well, take care, won't you?'

'Why are the police at your place?'

'They'll want to see us all, Trisha. Everyone who was associated with Keith. It's just something we have to accept, I guess. The people who worked with Keith probably knew him better than anyone except Rhelma. He didn't have many friends. There's always the chance, I suppose, that one of us might know something useful.'

After I had hung up I thought grimly: one of us might know something useful. Or one of us might have killed him.

I was genuinely not nervous about staying in the house. But I slept very little.

One sentence Martin had said kept going through my mind: He didn't have many friends. It was a sad epitaph for anyone, however true it may have been of the deliberately ill-mannered Keith who strove to keep people at a distance – and undoubtedly succeeded very well. But although he hadn't friends, how could he have made an enemy – one so ruthless as to kill him? What sort of person struck from behind at a defenceless man in a wheelchair?

A frightened person?

The thought leapt at me out of the darkness and I stopped tossing restlessly and thought about it for a long time. But in the end I had nothing but confused thoughts and eventually, towards dawn, I slept.

I woke while it was still very early, but when I slipped out to the kitchen Rhelma was already up and dressed, sitting at the table with a cup of coffee in front of her.

She smiled at me, her face still colourless, dark rings under her eyes. 'It was so good of you to stay, Trisha. It helped, just knowing you were here. I've phoned my sister in Brisbane. She's coming up later this morning, so I'll be all right. You must go to work. The rest of us have to go on living.'

She looked at me squarely. 'The police think I know why Keith was killed, even if I don't know who killed him. They're wrong. I don't know. I wish I did.' She paused a moment, looking off into some painful distance. 'The terrible thing is that perhaps I *should* know, and I don't.'

Eleanor phoned me at the factory office. I hardly believed it when she said, 'It's Eleanor West, Patricia. Would you come out to see me – whenever it's convenient?'

'Of course,' I said, trying not to sound startled. 'Would this afternoon after work be convenient for you?'

'Thank you,' she said, and hung up.

Periodically through the rest of the day that phone call kept pushing into my thoughts, puzzling me. Why would Eleanor, the silent recluse who avoided even her own family, want to see me?

When I drove up to the house Christine greeted me with a smile which had relief in it. 'When I heard the car I thought it would be the police again.'

'They've been here, I imagine?'

'Oh, yes. Talking to Gordon for ages this morning, asking me all manner of questions – can't imagine the reason for some of them. Neither Gordon nor I really have a solid alibi, either.' She gave a quick, unamused laugh. 'In future I think every time I go out alone or Gordon goes out and leaves me at home I'll be thinking of ways to prove where we both were. I mean, Gordon was at a meeting, but can't say precisely what time he left here, so he could have had time to go around and kill Keith. The children had gone home with a friend after school and stayed for tea because it was a birthday treat for the other child. I collected them about

eight-forty-five. So for about an hour *I* have no one to say
where I was or what I did. I don't suppose the police suspect
me. I don't suppose they suspect Gordon. But it gives you a
queer feeling when you've absolutely no proof you didn't do
it.'

I nodded. 'I know. I'm in the same situation. So is Nigel.
So is Martin – he'd arranged to play squash with a friend and
they had the court booked for eight, but Martin got a flat tyre
and had to change it on the way, so he was late. He said the
police got quite enthusiastic over that time-delay, but at least
he was able to show them the flat tyre, even though as he said
that still didn't prove anything because he had no proof of
when the flat tyre had happened. A couple of the other people
at the factory have pretty solid-looking alibis. Otto Klein is
vouched for by his wife, but I suppose alibis provided by a
person's family are always open to doubt.'

Christine said, 'Why do they think it was someone from the
factory, I wonder?'

I shrugged. 'I'm not sure they do. Not really. But the
motive evidently wasn't robbery, because Rhelma said nothing was missing as far as she could see, and nothing
disturbed. And, as Martin said, Keith didn't have many
friends, becuase he didn't associate with people. When you
don't associate with people you don't have much chance to
make enemies, either.'

'Nigel thinks Keith knew something about someone, and
that's why he was killed.'

'Well,' I said doubtfully, 'Keith liked to nose about. And he
liked to irritate people to see how they reacted. It was a form
of amusement to him, I think. But if he knew something
devastating about someone, why *tell* that person? Nothing
explains that.' I sighed. 'Oh, I don't know. It's all horrible.'

Christine said slowly, 'I can't help wondering if Rhelma
was the reason.'

I stared. 'Rhelma? She adored him!'

'No, no.' Christine shook her head. 'I don't mean she had
anything to do with it, or has the slightest idea why it

happened. But she's an attractive young woman. Suppose someone had a really big thing about her and knew it was quite hopeless because as long as Keith was around Rhelma would never look at anyone else.'

I was watching her intently.

She smiled faintly. 'No, I assure you I have no suspicions of anyone. But the thought occurred to me. And perhaps only because I so desperately want to think it had nothing to do with the factory. And the family.'

'Yes,' I agreed. 'I know what you mean. Which brings me to the purpose of my visit: Eleanor phoned and asked me to come to see her.'

'Eleanor!' Christine looked startled.

'I know. I was just as surprised. I've no idea what it's about. Have the police talked to her?'

'Oh, yes. She's probably the one of all of us who would have the nearest thing to an alibi: she has no car, and it's rather unlikely that she could have walked all the way from here to town and back without being seen and recognized. And quite apart from that she didn't know Keith Barnes and so would hardly have any reason to kill him.'

As I walked around to the door to Eleanor's flat I reflected that *someone* had had a reason to kill him, even though it might be difficult for us to imagine what the reason might be.

Eleanor opened the door at once in answer to my knock. 'Thank you for coming,' she said in that odd, expressionless manner I remembered. 'Please sit down.'

I had never been in her section of the house before. The living-room with its adjacent small kitchen was quite spacious and furnished with a grace and charm which somehow surprised me. It was dominated by a magnificent grand piano which stood open, sheets of music on the stand, as if in very frequent use. I realized the apartment was air-conditioned. Eleanor West did not have to suffer the intrusion of the outside world by even so much as an open window.

She sat down in an easy-chair facing mine, and suddenly I thought that although she was slender, there was no frailty about her. The tall figure was strong, no doubt from the many walks she apparently took, plus some gardening. I wondered what she thought about in all her solitary hours and days, this still-young woman who would be very attractive but for the strange immobility of face and the expressionless eyes.

'I have been told you and the widow of the murdered man are close friends,' she said without preamble.

'Rhelma and I are good friends, yes,' I agreed.

'Then I should be grateful if you can tell me whether now she might need financial assistance and if so how best I may provide it.'

It was so unexpected that I'm sure my jaw sagged slightly and left me open-mouthed.

'That's very kind of you,' I said warmly after a moment. 'I'm sure Rhelma will be most touched that – '

'You will not tell her.' The words were not quite curt, simply an order. 'It isn't a question of kindness. It is a responsibility. Selbridges looks after its employees. The company itself is not in a financial position to make an offer. I am. Does the woman need money?'

'I don't know,' I said. 'I think she will be all right, but I don't know. She's never talked of their financial situation. I'll find out – discreetly, I promise – and let you know.'

'You need not trouble to contact me unless she needs help,' Eleanor said coolly, and stood up with a curiously lithe movement.

Interview ended. I rose obediently and followed her to the door as she went to open it.

Then on a sudden impulse I said, 'Eleanor, you said you wanted Selbridges sold in order to be rid of anything which reminded you of Julian West. Then why do you keep this house?'

I waited, expecting my reckless query would meet with either an explosion of cold fury or icy, silent disdain.

Instead Eleanor paused, her back to me, her hand on the door-knob, and I saw her shoulders stiffen. There were perhaps twenty silent seconds.

'I don't know,' she said, and her voice was no longer expressionless, but tight with pain. 'I don't know. I wish to God I did.'

She pulled the door open almost violently and I went out. I didn't speak and she didn't look at me.

I went slowly through the garden, turning once to look back at the house. Although I hadn't really meant to ask the question it was one which frequently stirred in the back of my mind: why did she keep the house?

Surely, of all things, it was the one most guaranteed to remind her of Julian. When she had chosen the rooms to be turned into her self-contained flat, she had kept their bedroom: the room in which he had tried so horribly to murder her. All the joy of her love for him, all the agony of his treachery, was linked with that room, this house. Even if she felt she couldn't take the use of the house from Gordon and Christine while the Selbridge financial position was so precarious, she herself had money – Peter De Witt's money. She could well afford to simply *give* the house to Gordon, and go away to some place which held no nightmares.

Christine was doing some weeding in the front garden, making use of the last of the summer daylight. I hadn't yet become used to the shorter Queensland twilights, with night following so rapidly on the heels of sunset, unlike the long southern twilights I'd always known. I suspected Christine had deliberately chosen to be outdoors in order to find out why Eleanor had wanted to see me.

I told her, and added, 'Christine, it's none of my business, I know, but did Eleanor ever have her marriage to Julian annulled? I mean, she could have, after he'd been gone a year, couldn't she? Regardless of anything else?'

Christine looked at me curiously. 'Both Gordon and I advised her to, and I'm certain her solicitor did also. But she never did.'

'I see.' I turned again and looked back at the house. 'Why do you ask?'

'Don't you ever wonder why Eleanor goes on living here, in this house?'

'Often. But it's hardly something Eleanor is about to explain – if she knows.'

'I asked her, just now,' I said. 'I had absolutely no right to. It was just a sudden impulse and I asked before I thought. I expected she'd be furious.'

'She wasn't?'

I shook my head. 'She only said, in a strangely desperate kind of way: "I don't know. I wish to God I did." '

Sadness touched Christine's pleasant, good-humoured face. 'Poor Eleanor. She loved that rotten man so much.'

I said slowly, 'I had the oddest feeling, when I was talking to her. I think she half-expects him to come back. Perhaps half wants him to.'

Christine looked startled. 'She couldn't! Not after what he did to her. And certainly she'd know he'd never dare to come back.'

'I'm sure he wouldn't. But I did wonder whether Eleanor is as sure as you and I are.'

I went to bed that night feeling almost numb with weariness. The initial shock of learning about the murder, and the attendant sharply-awake feeling, had begun to wear off, leaving penetrating exhaustion. Martin phoned and asked if I'd like him to come around. I hesitated and he said gently, 'You're horribly tired, aren't you? You looked like a ghost at work today. Have an early night and just try to forget it all for a while. There's nothing more any of us can do at the moment. Rhelma's being cared for by her sister, and the rest of the wretched business is in the hands of the police. They're the experts.'

'I can't help thinking, wondering if there's something any of us *should* have noticed, should have guessed. But I've wondered so much my head's in a total whirl; and I *am* horribly tired.'

'Of course you are. Go get some sleep. You care too much about things for your own good. But then, that's what makes you what you are. And Trish?'

'Yes?'

'Not just now – not yet – but one day: will you marry me?'

I sat holding the phone for several seconds, a desire to laugh and cry and sing and dance all surging up from somewhere deep inside me in a great leaping wave, flinging weariness aside.

'What a time to ask me,' I said a trifle shakily. 'And what a way: by *telephone*?'

'Oh, well, it's better than nothing. I'll do much better than that some other time. I didn't mean to do it just at that moment – it just happened. Now go and get some sleep. Goodnight.'

And he hung up without giving me a chance to say another word.

I laughed out loud and said to the empty flat, 'What a *nut* I've fallen in love with!'

As I lay looking at the darkness through the kaleidoscope of thoughts which chased across my brain, something kept lurking just below the surface of conscious thought. Something which troubled me, and I became aware that I didn't want to think about it for some reason I didn't understand. It was something Christine had said, and eventually I made myself let the thought surface.

Christine had said she wondered if Rhelma might have been the reason for Keith's death: 'Suppose someone had a really big thing about her and knew it was quite hopeless because as long as Keith was around Rhelma would never look at anyone else.'

The thought disturbed me a great deal, but I had no real idea why. Had I, somewhere in my subconscious, wondered if Martin was attracted to Rhelma? Well, I could stop thinking that, now.

I smiled to myself as another thought occurred to me: he

hadn't waited to know if I would marry him. Presumably he was already quite sure. And on that thought sleep claimed me.

Eight

As he had promised, Martin did repeat his proposal much more forcefully, much more tenderly, and in much greater detail. And got the answer he expected. 'I can't marry you now,' he said. 'Not yet. I want you, need you, must have you. But I can't marry you yet. There are things I have to do – things I have to *be* – first.'

I said, my head against his shoulder, 'Why? What are you talking about?'

He took a long breath. 'My father was a labourer. He worked on the roads, dug ditches – literally. His only pleasure was to come home drunk out of his mind on Saturday nights. My mother had a lousy life. When I was still quite small I vowed I'd have something better – much better – for *my* wife. And I will. Something much better than being an accountant in someone else's company.' He chuckled. 'Even if it does give me the chance to marry the boss. Or one of them. Give me a year, and I'll be much more than a tame accountant in Selbridges.'

I sighed. 'What rubbish you talk.'

'Oh, no. It isn't rubbish. And I love you.'

And sometimes I felt that was the only sane thing in the days that followed Keith's death. The police kept turning up occasionally at the factory and once at my flat, asking all manner of questions about Keith, about Rhelma, about various staff members at Selbridges. They interviewed everyone from the factory, at work and at home, some of them over and over. Often the questions seemed totally irrelevant and irritating. They appeared to get nowhere. Someone had walked in off the street – presumably someone Keith knew and had admitted to the house though not necessarily so – killed him and walked out again, leaving no clue. Neighbours hadn't noticed or heard anything unusual.

Rhelma told me that the detective sergeant had admitted it was the most difficult kind of crime to solve.

'And yet,' Martin said to me thoughtfully, 'it wasn't a random killing. Or at least the odds against it are enormous.'

'How can you be sure?' I asked.

'Well, look at the facts. The door was probably unlocked, sure, so anybody *could* have got in. But that presupposes a madman with a sudden urge to kill just happened to choose one of the few houses in town whose front doors would be unlocked at that time of night, and found Keith sitting at the table, probably writing something. It mightn't have been impossible for the killer to sneak up behind him unheard. But that damned war-axe thing he was killed with was in a bracket on the wall where he'd have seen anyone who took it down. I asked Nigel about that – about the position of the wheelchair – and I imagine the police did also. And if Keith was writing something, what happened to it? Obviously the killer took it. It would seem Keith must have been either reading or writing, or he'd hardly have been sitting at that table. So whatever it was, it must have been something the murderer wanted, perhaps because it incriminated him.'

'Or her,' I said automatically.

Martin looked at me hard for a second. 'Or her,' he agreed. 'What I'm saying is that although it appears at first a *senseless* murder the evidence points to the fact that there must have been a reason. If the police could uncover the reason there's a much better chance of identifying the murderer. In a case like this where no clues are left, no mistakes made, unless the motive is known the chances of finding the killer aren't good, to say the least.'

'You mean you think they might never find out who killed him? But that's horrible!'

'It's happened before today, often enough,' he said grimly.

I felt perhaps Rhelma shared his feeling. It was natural enough that she should be deeply shocked and grieved. But as the days ran into weeks there seemed to be a strange quality about her not entirely explained by sorrow or a sense of loss. She seemed to me somehow *watchful*. I could think of no other word to describe it. It seemed to me that she believed Keith's murderer was someone she knew, and if she were alert enough she might catch that person out. It distressed me to think what it must be like for her: on top of her grief she had to live with the knowledge that perhaps some hand held out to her with murmured words of sympathy had held the axe that ended Keith's life; some friend who smiled at her was no friend.

She didn't appear to have any suspicion of me, but I couldn't really know even that, and it was a rather strange feeling when I was with her. She always seemed glad to see me, and after a few weeks we resumed our habit of going riding together, particularly when Martin was out on his deep-sea fishing trips or was at one or other of the beaches, surf-board riding, at which he was very skilled. Rhelma had indicated in answer to my cautious questioning that she could cope financially, so I had no occasion to see Eleanor again.

Christmas and New Year slipped by with everyone connected with the factory still in a somewhat subdued mood, though Gordon and Christine made it as festive as possible for the sake of the children.

I remember it was a hot, humid day in mid-January, a blue sky piled high with cumulus clouds that presaged the onset of the rainy season, when I noted a letter from New Zealand was amongst the mail I routinely put on Gordon's desk.

He brought it back to me a while later. 'This is interesting, Trisha.' There was a note of near-excitement in his voice. 'It just could be a real chance to broaden our markets.'

The letter from an Auckland retailer expressed interest in Selbridge furniture 'following the letter from your sales manager', and said their company, with outlets in four major New Zealand cities, would be interested to receive further details.

I looked up at Gordon. 'Did you know Martin had contacted this company?'

'He spoke to me a little time ago about the prospect of trying a New Zealand market. I gave him the addresses of two or three firms, but I didn't really expect results. We must have a conference when Nigel and Martin are available and decide the best approach.'

Somewhat to my surprise, they all agreed that a pesonal approach was justified, though Nigel seemed fractionally less enthusiastic than Gordon and Martin. It seemed to me a considerable expense for a struggling company, but I could see the merit of the idea.

'It's a chance to expand markets,' Gordon said, 'and it's well worth a few hundred dollars to do that. You're the sales manager, Martin, and you made the initial contact, so I'd suggest you should be the one to go.'

'Nigel's the designer,' Martin said. 'If these people have any ideas about specific designs or trends he can handle it better than anyone. How are the designs for those two new lines coming along, Nigel?'

Nigel looked at me with his slow grin. 'Trish has been advising me on the space-age stuff. Most of her advice has been to burn the plans, certainly, but given another week I might convince even her. In actual fact, she's made some very good suggestions of a more constructive nature. She has a natural flair for furniture design.'

I raised my eyebrows. 'You never mentioned it, to put it mildly.'

We had been engaging for weeks past in running verbal battles over his new designs, hurling insults at each other almost constantly but, I had to admit, without the slightest rancour. I had found his strange ultra-streamlined chairs and sofas and tables, which would look at home in some science-fiction film of the twenty-fifth century, too weird and outrageously innovative for my taste. But their starkly-clean lines had a way of growing on me, and when he had produced what he called a prototype chair I had to admit it was remarkably comfortable.

The other new line he had been developing was what he called 'country-style furniture as it never was but should have been'. It had a rugged, chunky, durable look – a look that somehow suggested pipe-smoke and a fire in the grate, a large dog sprawled on a rug and a general air of a secure retreat from a cold, wet outside world. It certainly didn't belong in an elegant drawing-room, but I liked it – and it, too, had the body-supporting immense comfort I had come to recognize as the real worth of Selbridge furniture.

'If I'd told you that you had a talent for design you'd have elbowed me aside and taken over my drawing-board,' Nigel said. 'Anyway, I can have those designs finished and a couple of pieces made in a week if nothing urgent crops up, so I could include photographs of those in the stuff to show this Auckland fellow.'

'Right,' Gordon said firmly. 'I'll write him that you'll arrive in a week.'

But the day before he was to go, Nigel went down with severe flu. 'You'd better go after all, Martin,' Gordon said.

Martin pulled a wry face. 'Sorry. Would you believe I don't have a current passport?' He looked at me. 'What about Trish? You have a current passport, don't you? I remember you telling me you'd been to New Zealand eighteen months ago.'

'Well, yes, but how can *I* go? I'm a raw recruit in the furniture business.'

'You did all the checking on import-export regulations, Customs rules and all that. Plus you're always arguing with Nigel over his designs, so you must know a great deal about them by now. And I think what he said was right: you have a natural feel for what makes good furniture.'

'Exactly. It's ideal. Besides, you're just the thing to charm some hard-headed businessman.' Gordon looked at me with twinkling eyes.

'Thanks,' I said dryly. 'I've never sold anything in my life.'

Martin said firmly, 'Gordon's right: you stand a better chance than any of us. Well, don't just stand there, girl,' he grinned. 'You've a lot to do before you catch that plane tomorrow.'

'You're not wrong,' I said glumly.

He laughed. 'No sense of adventure, that's your problem. Anyway, I know Nigel had everything pretty well organized. He's got a briefcase absolutely bulging with sketches and photographs and fabric samples and heaven knows what.'

Rhelma volunteered to drive me to the airport. 'It'll do me good,' she said, 'and save taking anyone away from the factory.'

She picked me up from my flat and we called at the factory to pick up Nigel's briefcase of material, which I hadn't been able to have before because Gordon had been working on some last-minute costings to include on the newest lines. As I hurried back to the car Otto Klein called from the doorway of the upholstery section: 'Good luck, Miss Kent!'

I turned and waved and, turning back, tripped over a hose I hadn't noticed lying across the path. I stumbled and almost fell and, remembering in some alarm that some ornamental shrubs beside the path were supported by metal stakes, I instinctively put my hands in front of me, fearful of falling on one. All that happened was that I caught the bottom of Nigel's briefcase on one of the stakes and then I had recovered my balance. But somehow it just seemed to me that the tiny mishap was some kind of omen that my trip was going to be, at best, a failure.

'Are you all right?' Rhelma asked as I slid into the car. 'You could have given your hand a nasty cut on that steel post.'

'I'm fine. It was so silly – just clumsy.' I laughed. I was determined not to let Rhelma see my mood was one of pessimism if not actual foreboding. She had enough very real worries. She didn't want to be burdened with my fanciful ones.

But the flight across the Tasman was smooth and I spent most of the time going through the sketches and diagrams of frames and bracing of the furniture pieces; photographs of completed furniture; samples of fabrics and leathers; even the samples of the timber involved, polished to show the beauty of grain. And interest in it absorbed me again, and when the plane landed in Auckland under a clear blue afternoon sky my spirits had begun to revive considerably, and by the time I left my hotel next morning to interview our prospective client I was, if not precisely optimistic, at least determined to do my best by Selbridge Furniture.

My interview was with the general manager of the furniture retail chain. He was a big, hawk-eyed man who seemed unnervingly incapable of smiling, though he was unfailingly courteous, even to taking me to a charming little café for coffee. He explained that he would have to consult with his sales manager and they would both need more time to study the material; would I come back to see him again tomorrow? I certainly would.

And on the following day, to my near-astonishment, he handed me an order which was quite sizeable. 'You will realize,' he said, 'that this has to be in the nature of a trial shipment. We have to test market reaction. And we have placed certain conditions – to which I hope your company will agree – that particular lines purchased by us will not be made available to any other retailers in this country.'

'I don't think there'll be any problems in that,' I said. 'Selbridge furniture isn't exactly mass-produced.'

'So I would imagine. However, it seems only fair to point out to you that there is to be a furniture trade exhibition here about the middle of this year. I can put you in touch with some of the people organizing it, if you have time to talk to them. Your company might consider exhibiting.'

I thanked him, feeling guilty over my initial impression that he was a cold and unhelpful fish, and by the time I flew home the next day, armed with the provisional order and details and encouragement from the organizers of the forth-coming furniture trade exhibition, I was in a mood of elation that was in sharp contrast with my gloomy premonitions when I had left home.

It was sunny when the plane left Auckland, but less than half-way across the Tasman we came upon heavy cloud below us, and when we landed in Brisbane it was teeming with rain. Martin met me and was exuberant with delight when I told him the outcome of the trip while we had coffee at the airport, and all the way home he plied me with questions.

'You could have telelphoned,' he complained. 'Every-body's been on tenterhooks – what's a tenterhook, I wonder? – and I think Gordon's almost had a nervous collapse. Not to mention I've practically developed an ulcer.'

Nigel alone among the members of the company seemed somewhat less than delighted. Christine and Rachael had come in to the factory office to hear my report of the outcome of the trip. Nigel sat almost silent while I talked and everyone plied me with questions in a general air of much satisfaction and enthusiasm. When I had a chance to speak to Nigel alone, I said, 'Aren't you pleased?'

'Of course,' he said.

'You don't seem especially enthusiastic. Don't you feel it's an important breakthrough – Selbridges' first international sale? Surely it's a real step towards consolidating the com-pany?'

He looked at me steadily, rather searchingly, for several sconds. Then he smiled. 'Sorry I haven't sounded very bright. Put it down to just getting over the flu. Yes, of course it sounds very good for Selbridges. You did a first-rate job. But – well, it's just a beginning. Let's hope it goes well.'

'Why shouldn't it?' I persisted. 'Ours *is* good furniture, isn't it?'

'Yes,' he said. 'It's very good.'

And then Martin came over to ask me something frivolous about New Zealand weather and I had no further chance to wonder whether something about the deal was worrying Nigel, or had disappointed him. In any case, he had made it pretty clear he wasn't going to talk about it.

'New Zealand weather was superb compared with this,' I told Martin, nodding at the window where rain streamed steadily down the outside of the glass. 'How long has it been like this?'

'Just started yesterday. But it's the wet season here now, you know, so we can expect lots of this sort of thing till about the end of March.'

'Oh, great,' I said. 'Somebody should have told me before I left Victoria. Though I have to admit at least this rain is warm, not like the southern winter stuff. But heavens, look at it! Till the end of March, did you say? It looks as though it could go clear through till then without stopping.'

In fact, it stopped early on Saturday morning, and the sun came out in a clearing sky and blazed down in brilliant, steamy heat. Christine and Gordon had invited me out to dinner the previous evening and because the rain was so heavy Christine had insisted I stay overnight rather than drive back to my flat in the dark. We were just about to have breakfast when Wendy and Ken, who had been out early to feed the horse and generally relish the thought that it was going to be a fine day, came dashing in excitedly.

'Mum, Dad, come and look! There's a big hole in the ground in the side garden.'

Gordon sighed. 'Bandicoots been digging up the lawn again? They're nice little animals and I don't begrudge them the chance to rummage around the garden after beetles and things, but I wish they didn't do it with quite so much enthusiasm.'

'No, Dad,' Wendy said, with all the patience of a ten-year-old explaining the perfectly obvious. 'Not bandicoots. An *enormous* hole. The ground's just fallen in. It goes right back towards the side fence.'

'You could put a *car* in it,' Ken declared. 'Well, nearly.'

Gordon raised his eyebrows. 'Well, maybe we'd better have a look.'

There was indeed a considerable subsidence of earth just outside Eleanor's suite of rooms.

'I'll be darned!' Gordon said. 'That must be the old cellar.' He turned to me. 'The original owners of this place tried to establish a vineyard,' he explained. 'They had a wine-press in a shed there near the fence, and a cellar with entrances from the kitchen as well as the shed. Of course the project never got off the ground, because the climate and the soil didn't really suit grapes – especially the climate.'

'Yes,' I said. 'I remember the children telling me about the vineyard when I first came here.'

'The place was known for years as Farnhams' Folly, after the people who built it, or so the story goes,' Gordon added. 'Of course, that was a long time ago, but my father remembered it from when he was a small boy. The Farnhams had turned to some more practical kind of farming by then.'

'But Julian had that old cellar filled in when the renovations were made to the house and he and Eleanor were first married,' Christine said. 'I remember him and Eleanor talking about it at the time. The cellar hadn't been used for many years and was unsafe, so they decided to have it filled in.'

Gordon poked at the loose earth at the edge of the collapsed trench-like area with the toe of his shoe.

'Julian and Eleanor may have left *instructions* for it to be filled in,' he said, 'but remember the contractors who did the renovations did their work during the two or three months that Julian and Eleanor spent overseas on their extended honeymoon. The fellows obviously decided they could cut corners by not bothering to do a very thorough job of filling in a hole in the ground that was never likely to bother anyone – probably reckoned if it was boarded up at each end it'd be perfectly safe and no one was ever likely to know they hadn't actually done what they'd been paid to do.

It's only the really heavy rain of the past few days that proved too much for the poor old cellar.'

'Gosh, just think,' Ken mourned. 'It was here all the time and we didn't know. It would've been a fantastic place to play all kind of games and stuff.'

'Except for the fact you couldn't get in,' Gordon pointed out, 'and it would have been far too dangerous even if you could have. Come to think of it,' he added to Christine, 'a certain amount of earth fill had to be dumped into a subsidence when the remains of the old shed were bulldozed away – and that was after very heavy rain, too. I guess that should have told us the filling-in hadn't been too well carried out.'

'Everyone had a good many other things on their minds at the time,' Christine said. She added to me, 'That shed where the old wine-press had been was blown down in the storm the night of the fire, when Eleanor almost died.'

We all glanced instinctively at the door which led to Eleanor's flat, and as if on cue the door opened and Eleanor came out.

'What is it?' she asked, and then she saw the cave-in. 'Oh,' she said, almost disinterestedly.

Gordon explained what he believed had happened. 'I think we should ask Nigel to come out and have a look,' he added, 'because I should think there's some degree of risk it might have done some damage to the foundations of the house, especially along your wall. He's an architect. He'll know the best way to set about repairs.'

Eleanor nodded briefly. 'Whatever you think best,' she said, and went back into her rooms.

Nigel arrived in about an hour, and agreed that there had never been a real attempt to fill in the cellar. 'See,' he said, pointing. 'You can still see bits of the timber shoring on the walls and roof. Maybe they dumped some earth at each end and left the rest. I think it would be a good idea to get a back-hoe in and clear the whole lot away so it can be filled in properly, but most importantly so that I can get a good look at the house foundations. I'll phone a fellow I know – I think he'll be willing to do it even though it is Saturday morning.'

The back-hoe operator said he would be out shortly, and I had to confess to a curiosity scarcely less than the children's, and stayed to watch the operation. Wendy and Ken were slightly sorrowful that they had promised to go swimming with some of their school friends, but in the humid heat of the morning and the boredom of waiting for the excavating machine to arrive, they decided a swim was more appealing, and went off.

Nigel stayed to supervise the excavating, because it would require very careful work near the wall of the house where, as he said, he really didn't have much idea of what the situation would be at that side of the cellar, since that must be where the entry to the house had been.

Gordon had gone into town and Christine was busy in the house. To my surprise, Eleanor came out to watch as the clawing bucket on the mechanical arm of the back-hoe, skilfully operated, lifted out earth and shoring timbers and galvanized iron sheeting that had lined the earthen roof for waterproofing. It very rapidly became clear that the cellar – apart from the end at the site of the shed, where it had been properly filled in after the shed had been blown down – was in remarkably good condition.

Most of it was not even caved in, though there was an obviously-old earthfall near the house. But between that and the fresh earthfall of the previous night it had been virtually intact, with walls and roof still standing and neat flagstones paving the floor. Certainly no one had ever attempted to fill it in.

I turned to Eleanor. 'I don't understand. I thought Gordon said the house-entrance to the cellar was in the kitchen? But the kitchen isn't even on this side of the house.'

Eleanor said briefly, 'No. The house was all altered after I bought it. What was originally the kitchen became the main

bedroom – my bedroom now. I never saw just what the
entrance to the cellar was like – a trap-door type of thing, I
believe.'

I looked at the house. 'I suppose it must have been,
because an upright door would have had to open into a kind
of alcove above steps, and that would have meant a double
wall, and there isn't – '

The back-hoe driver gave a wordless shout and stopped
his machine and leapt to the ground, staring into the
excavation where he had just lifted away a section of the
cellar roof.

'What's wrong?' Nigel asked as we went to see.

The driver looked up, shock in his eyes. 'Best keep the
ladies back,' he said.

But beside me I heard Eleanor draw a sharp breath as we
both saw what was on the cellar floor.

A skeleton lay face down, draped with a few remnants of
clothing: dark trousers, what had probably been a
shower-proof jacket, a leather belt, shoes – all ragged with
decay. A watch was still around the left wrist, a dull gleam of
gold from a ring showed on the left hand, a torch lay near
the other outflung arm. There was no need to wonder how
he had died. A heavy beam, long fallen, lay across the back
of the skull, crushing it.

Nigel dropped down into the trench, which was some ten
feet deep, almost as if he felt some need to help, even though
it was years too late. Slowly he knelt on one knee beside the
body, just staring at it. Then carefully, I thought almost
reverently, he picked up something – it looked like a nail –
from beside the body and put it in his pocket almost as if he
felt no rubbish should be left there to desecrate the man's
remains. Then he got to his feet, standing quite still, never
taking his eyes off the man on the flagstoned floor.

Stunned and uncomprehending, I turned to Eleanor.
'Who on earth – ' I began, and stopped seeing her face.

There was no horror on her face as she gazed at the body,

only a strange look of wonder, even though she was marble-pale.

'Julian,' she whispered. 'Julian. May God forgive me.'

Nine

'Julian!' Shock jolted the word out of me and I whirled to look down at Nigel questioningly.

He looked up and met my eyes and nodded.

Instinctively I went to Eleanor and flung my arms around her. 'Come inside,' I said.

She let me take her arm and walk in with her. I sat her on the little sofa in her living-room and sat beside her without a word, my mind so full of confusion I had no idea what to think, let alone what to say.

I put my hand on hers and she turned and put her face on my shoulder and began to cry, silent sobs shaking her whole body as if all the bitter, unshed tears of the past two and a half years sought release. I just held her wordlessly, a thousand questions shouting in my brain for answers, all secondary to the terrible need this woman had for comfort that I couldn't give, though I dimly perceived her tears might.

Nigel, grim-faced, came to the door. 'Is she all right?' he asked.

I nodded.

'I'll call the police,' he said quietly, and went.

Christine, looking a shade pale but with her composure intact, came in a couple of minutes later with a glass in her hand. 'Nigel just told me,' she said, and then, like me, she just sat quietly and waited for the storm of sobbing to pass from Eleanor.

Presently she took a long shuddering breath and sat erect,

covering her face with her hands for a few moments.

'I brought you some brandy,' Christine said gently. 'I think you should drink it.'

'Thank you.' She took the glass in a slightly unsteady hand, but in her face there was a look of someone who has wakened from a nightmare, and found peace.

Neither Christine nor I spoke while she slowly drank the brandy. Then she put the glass down on a coffee table and looked from one to the other of us.

'Where's Nigel?'

'He's gone to phone the police,' Christine said. 'There'll be all sorts of formalities, I'm afraid.'

'Yes, of course.' Eleanor nodded.

I said slowly, 'I simply don't understand. I'm sorry,' I added to Eleanor. 'I guess it's the last thing you want to talk about.'

She shook her head and gave me a little smile. 'No. I want to talk about it. I want to tell the *world* about it.'

I must have looked bewildered.

'Don't you see? Julian didn't try to kill me. The fire, the sleeping-pills – all that was an accident, just as I said in the beginning. I must have taken the maximum dose of sleeping-pills, because I wasn't feeling well, and I always slept badly when Julian wasn't there. Then when I was getting hazy with drowsiness I must have forgotten I'd taken them, and took more. I usually had a cigarette before I went to bed. Being stupid with a double dose of sleeping-pills, I evidently knocked the ashtray into the waste-paper basket, with the still-burning cigarette-butt in it. Mrs Marsh was wrong about the door. It did tend to catch sometimes in wet weather, and she was panicking.'

She paused, looking off into the distance as if she were watching it all happening.

'He must have been on his way back from finding that the people he'd gone to visit were out. He would have seen the fire behind the window as he came into the drive, and he'd have known it was my room – our room. He would have heard Mrs Marsh screaming that the door was locked and wouldn't open. To break down one of these doors would be very difficult – they're solid oak and they have particularly heavy locks – so he must have decided to risk trying to get through the old cellar. Evidently he'd found out nothing had been done about filling it in. He wouldn't have mentioned it for fear the children – Wendy and Ken, or any children, for that matter – might try going into it when they were here on a visit. That was the main reason he was anxious to have it done away with in the first place – the fear that children might try adventuring in there and come to harm from a cave-in of walls or roof.'

Nigel had come in quietly. Eleanor didn't seem to notice him. She was far too intent on her thoughts.

'He was prepared to risk a cave-in of the cellar, and the fire itself,' she said. 'He got almost to the house, and the beam fell, and killed him. And all this time I have believed he tried to kill me.'

Her eyes were dark with the pain of grief.

'We're all equally guilty of misjudging him,' Christine said. 'Don't blame yourself.'

'But he was my husband. He was – he was Julian. I should have known. I should always have known.'

Nigel put his arm around her shoulders. 'You only believed what intelligent thought forced you to believe,' he told her. 'You accepted the evidence. Julian would never blame you for that.'

She looked at him with a quick smile. 'I know. But all the time he was just – there.' She glanced out at the garden. 'Nigel, it would have been – quick, wouldn't it?'

He nodded. 'Instant. He'd never have known what happened.' He hesitated. 'I had to call the police, Eleanor. They'll be out in a few minutes. I'm sorry, but it had to be done. There'll be all the formalities to go through, I'm afraid, and the influx of the curious, the media and so on. We'll try to keep them away as much as possible.'

She shook her head. 'That's all right. I don't mind. I'll

talk to anyone who'll go out – ' her voice almost broke, but she quickly recovered ' – and tell the world that my husband was no murderer; he was the bravest of men. Far from trying to kill me, he gave his life in a bid to save me.'

We all fell silent. I couldn't know exactly what the others were thinking, but I was thinking of Aunt Agnes: remembering her voice saying, 'Your cousin Julian's the pick of the lot of them.' Remembering the wedding photograph of the handsome, blue-eyed man with the laughter in his face, and Eleanor so transparently happy on his arm. Well, after all, Eleanor and Aunt Agnes had been right.

The police came, followed by an ambulance. The police didn't ask Eleanor many questions, but contented themselves with taking measurements and many photographs before they lifted away the beam and the ambulance men went down into the cellar to carefully remove the remains.

Christine and I stayed with Eleanor, and when the ambulance had gone the two detectives and the two uniformed men who had come in answer to Nigel's phone call, came to the door. One of them was Detective Sergeant Cunningham, who had investigated Keith Barnes's murder.

'I'm so very sorry to intrude, Mrs West,' he said to Eleanor, 'but I must ask if you know the whereabouts of the entrance to the cellar from your room. If you don't feel you can put up with us prowling about today we can come back tomorrow.'

'It's quite all right, Sergeant,' Eleanor said. 'I don't know where the door is, or even if it really still exists. Obviously my husband either knew or hoped it did, but he hadn't mentioned it for the reasons I spoke of earlier.' She smiled. 'He may even have feared *I* might be tempted to do some exploring for myself, and I have to admit he was probably right. By all means try to locate the door. I should be most interested to find it myself.'

Eleanor's bedroom was quite a large room, the window whose curtain had been set alight by the burning waste-paper basket no longer crossed by security bars. The floor was carpeted and there was an *ensuite* and a walk-in wardrobe.

Nigel and Gordon had come in with the policemen, and Nigel said, 'It must be a trap-door type of entrance in the floor, or there'd be an indication of double walls. Most probably it's against an outer wall, but not necessarily so.'

They all went around tapping at the floor in an effort to pick up a hollow sound to indicate the floor wasn't solid at that point. It was one of the uniformed men who presently said, 'Here, Sergeant. There's something here.'

In the floor of the section of the walk-in wardrobe which was empty and so presumably had been Julian's, a handle which looked like a double piece of skirting-board slid, after some considerable struggling, to allow a small trap-door to be opened. Stone steps led down, and then the whole thing was blocked by fallen earth and rubble.

'So he couldn't have got in anyway,' Eleanor said very quietly.

Sergeant Cunningham looked at her. 'That earthfall might have occurred *since* the night your husband was killed, Mrs West. But we think – and both your brother' – he nodded at Nigel – 'and the back-hoe driver agree with us, and they are rather more expert in this sort of thing – that this fall of earth actually occurred as your husband was coming along through the cellar. It appears that it was this subsidence, which is mainly outside the house-floor area, which caused the beam to fall on Mr West. The violent storm of that night – heavy rain and high wind combined with a severe electrical storm – may very well have been the thing which triggered it. The shed, where the other opening to the cellar was, was blown down in that storm, I understand.'

Eleanor nodded.

'Quite possibly the fact that the shed collapsed might have caused sufficient of a jolt to loosen some earth and cause the section of cellar wall to crumble and bring the beam down, and block the entrance to the house. Or it may have been due to your husband inadvertently loosening something by stumbling over fallen timbers or bumping against a wall.

And Mr Selbridge tells me that earth and rock was dumped into the apparent subsidence where the shed had stood.'

He didn't add that it was this fact that the cellar was sealed off at each end which had effectivly entombed the body so that no evidence of its presence would have reached anyone. 'There'll be an inquest,' he said. 'But it will be little more than a formality. There has to be positive identification of the body, but your husband's dentist will have records which will make that simple enough. There shouldn't be any undue delay in enabling you to make funeral arrangements.'

I began to feel I was an outsider intruding on a family bereavement, and I went outside. I tried to wander around the garden, but the presence of that cellar was too much for me and I had to go back and stare at it. The back-hoe driver hadn't gone away, but was tinkering with his machine, and I realized with a little shock that the work he had come to do still had to be done. Once the police had finished with the area – and presumably they had, by now – the place where Julian West's body had lain would finally be cleared of rubble, any necessary repairs to the foundations of the house would be done, and the hole in the ground where the cellar had been would be filled with rock and earth. It would all be tidy again.

'Trisha.' It was Martin's voice beside me, and his arms went tightly around me.

I had never needed him so much. I put my face against him and began to cry. In a moment I pulled myself up and wiped my eyes. 'Sorry. A bit silly, isn't it? To cry for a man I didn't even know.'

Martin's dark eyes watched me with a gentle smile. 'It seems no one knew him. Except Eleanor, of course.'

I nodded. 'How did you know? About all this?'

'Nigel phoned me. I think he felt you'd had a bit of a shock, and might like a bit of support. He said you'd been looking after Eleanor.'

I shook my head wonderingly. 'Somehow I think Eleanor has suddenly become stronger than any of us.'

Over the days that followed, through the legal formalities, the curiosity, the media interest, the friends who came with genuine sympathy, I think no one could fail to marvel at the transformation of Eleanor.

The tight-faced, weary-eyed recluse, embittered and silent, was suddenly a poised, charming, beautiful woman, grieving, but with her face alight with pride in the man she had loved. The man she and everyone else had believed so treacherous and evil was now revealed as a brave man who had died in a desperate attempt to save her life. The years of avoiding people were over. As she had said, she didn't mind the sensation this had created; she would talk to reporters or anyone else who would spread the truth about Julian.

Dental records having established positive identification and pathology tests having confirmed the obvious cause of death, the funeral could be held, and Julian West was laid in a flower-decked plot on a gentle hillside in the town's garden cemetery, while honey-eaters flitted in and out among crimson callistemons beside the path and higher on the hill a magpie announcing his nesting-site declared to the world in rippling song his faith in life.

Afterwards, Christine came to me. 'Mother and Nigel are coming back to the house with us and staying for dinner. Eleanor would like you and Martin to come, too – and so would Gordon and I.'

I hesitated, fearing to intrude, and Christine smiled. 'Please say yes. The children have found it all a bit sobering, after the first excitement, and they really enjoy having you around. And Eleanor meant it when she said she would like you to come.'

Martin and I entertained the children out of doors for a time to allow the adult members of the family and a couple of their close friends, who had also come back to the house briefly, time together in private. The children were rather subdued at first, but when Martin began admiring Dobby, their elderly horse, and seriously discussing the finer equine points as he would with a fellow-breeder, they returned to their normal high spirits.

Martin and I were the only non-family members at dinner. It was a pleasant, surprisingly relaxed meal, with Eleanor readily joining in the general conversation, and only Nigel seemed unusually quiet. The meal over, the children went off to read or watch television.

Gordon stood up, his glass in his hand, his face serious.

'Before we all go our separate ways,' he said quietly, 'if you'll excuse the formality, I would like to propose a toast.'

He looked around the table at us all. 'To the memory of a man we have all wronged in our minds and with our words. He gave his life in an act of great courage. Let's drink to Julian.'

We stood and raised our glasses. There was nothing bizarre about it. It was just a simple act of honouring a man who had been cruelly misjudged, and I found it deeply moving.

As we sat down there was a moment of silence and Eleanor looked steadily at Nigel.

'Don't you think,' she said, 'that that was rather a mockery on your part?'

We all stared at her, dumbfounded. I glanced at Nigel. A flicker of shock showed for a moment in his face, and then he merely raised one eyebrow enquiringly.

Eleanor's voice was more sad than accusing. 'You have let him be thought a thief all this time. I suppose you felt it was a small thing to add to the crime he was suspected of. I don't find it hard to forgive you for taking the money. You were going through a bad time, and we all know you've repaid the money and more by the work you've done for a pittance. Taking the money was one thing. Letting Julian accept the blame is something else.'

Nigel sat quite still for a long moment. Then he got up unhurriedly and walked out without a word.

Everyone was awkwardly silent, and I followed Nigel as he strode out to his car.

I caught his arm. 'Eleanor didn't mean it. She was upset, that's all.'

He turned to look at me. I couldn't see his excpression in the light from the house windows.

'Everyone means it,' he said. 'Eleanor's the only one who's said it, that's all. Oh, I've seen them looking at me in a funny way at times since Julian was found. Because one of us took the money. While Julian was the villain it was easy for everyone to believe he was the one who embezzled the firm. Now he's a hero, so he can't also be a thief. That leaves only me.'

'You're not a thief.'

'Nice of you to say so, but don't try to convince the others.'

'But why does it have to be either you or Julian? Why not someone else – some other employee?'

'Because it had to be someone with access to the money and the books. That meant someone in the family. Who? Gordon was in Brisbane most of the time, Eleanor didn't work in the business; Mother worked there part time only. Can you imagine any of them in the role of embezzler? Use your intelligence, girl, and don't go around believing the best of everybody.'

'The fact that Julian was a very brave man with a good deal of daring in him doesn't prove he wasn't also an embezzler.'

'As I said, don't try to convince the others of that.'

'But – '

'Leave it!'

He turned on me, suddenly, startlingly. Involuntarily I took a step back.

Then he shook his head, looking tired. 'Look, if you think I'm not a thief, thank you. I mean it. But just – leave it. The family aren't going to press charges. I imagine it will never be mentioned again – certainly not in my hearing, even by Eleanor.'

And he got into his car and drove away.

Ten

By the time I went back into the dining-room the incident seemed to have been totally dismissed and the conversation was general and normal. Martin and I left soon afterwards and neither of us mentioned it as he drove me home. As he saw me into my flat, he looked down at me with that quizzical twinkle in his brown eyes that I knew so well.

'Not the best night to ask if you want me to stay, I guess,' he said.

'Not really. And stop looking at me like that. When you do my blood turns to fire and my bones to water, if you'll excuse the cliché.'

He grinned. 'Who cares about the cliché? I must just remember the technique.' He laid one hand gently on my cheek. 'You look truly weary. Get a good night's sleep. Are you and Rhelma going to ride my overweight nags for me tomorrow?'

'Yes, if the weather holds. It looks as if it's building up to some rain again. You're going down to the Gold Coast tomorrow, aren't you? Board-riding?'

'I think so. The surf down there's supposed to be very good just now, and it's pretty poor here at the moment. I want to get in some practice for the competition next month. But I'll stay here if you'd rather I didn't go.'

I shook my head. 'Don't be silly. You love it, and I'll enjoy my day with Rhelma.'

Martin was right: I was bone-weary. But the events of the day – and of the past week or so – combined with the hot, oppressive night, made me restless. When Martin had gone I tried to read for a while, because I was much too wide awake and my mind in far too much turmoil to make sleep a possibility. I couldn't concentrate on reading, and soon put the book aside and made myself a cup of coffee. I sat sipping it and thinking of the factory.

I had begun to find that the longer I worked in the factory, the greater the importance Selbridge Furniture assumed in my life. At the oddest times I would find myself thinking about furniture designs, and how this chair would look in that fabric or what would be the best kind of wood for a particular table.

By the time I had finished my second cup of coffee I knew it was no use: I wasn't going to sleep. My mind was full of thoughts about Julian West, about Eleanor and about Nigel. And I didn't want to think any more about any of them. The only thing that might let me put them out of my mind would be to go to the factory and put in a couple of hours' work in the office. There was some business correspondence to be caught up with. I could do that. And by then I might be so tired I would sleep anyway. I picked up my keys and went out to the car.

Something about the air seemed in keeping with my restless mood: it was dead calm, but so heavy with moist heat it was opressive and almost threatening.

I let myself into the factory, switching on lights as I went, and settled myself down in the office to concentrate on the lagging correspondence. I typed up two or three letters for Gordon to sign on Monday, and then discovered that before answering the next I needed some information that was in with the material I'd taken to New Zealand, and I gloomily predicted to myself that by now Nigel would have reclaimed his briefcase and probably taken it and all its contents home.

But it was still in the office cupboard where I had put it, and I was able to finish all the waiting corrspondence, by which time it was long after midnight and I tidied up my desk with the contented feeling that I could now go home and sleep: doing routine chores had helped my brain shed some of its disturbing thoughts over things that were out of my control anyway. As I picked up the briefcase to put it away again I smiled a little to myself at the memory of the gloomy frame of mind in which I had set out on that sales trip to New Zealand, and how events had proved my premonitions of failure to be nonsense – like most premonitions.

I recalled I'd forgotten to apologize to Nigel for damaging his briefcase by catching it on that metal garden-post the morning I was leaving. I must tell him about that – not that the damage was any more than purely superficial, but I'd been brought up to have great respect for other people's property, and it was something ingrained in my nature from childhood. Automatically I ran my hand along the underside of the case to feel the little cut in the vinyl.

There was no cut.

For a moment it didn't register. I just slid my hand along the surface again, thinking I'd missed it. Then I turned the case on its side and looked at it. There was no scratch. The case was quite undamaged.

I sat down slowly, a tingling chill creeping through my nerves.

I made myself check the case over methodically, carefully – both case and contents. It was a perfectly ordinary heavy brown vinyl briefcase with Nigel's initials, N.P.S., in one corner. A tiny part of my mind, probably because I didn't want to face the implications of the whole thing, wondered absurdly what the P stood for. The contents were exactly as they should have been – even to one of my handkerchiefs. This was most certainly the briefcase I had brought back from New Zealand.

But it was not the one I had taken over.

I sat for a long time, just looking at it, feeling very close to fear. Someone had used me as a courier for some purpose that was certainly illegal and possibly evil. There was no other explanation. Whoever that person was, it was someone connected with Selbridge Furniture.

Anger flared up in me, replacing the shock. Someone had played me for a sucker. In all innocence I had taken some kind of contraband across the Tasman, cheerfully carried it through Customs checks. And if it had been detected, I was the one who'd be facing charges while the guilty party stayed safe and untouchable.

What had I taken to New Zealand? Or what had I brought back?

I had emptied everything out of the briefcase, and now I examined it painstakingly. There was no deception – no secret compartments, no false bottom. But of course I couldn't say that of the case I'd taken over, because naturally I hadn't looked at it with a suspicious eye. Also, it was quite possible that there *had* been some kind of removable inner lining in this case, and whoever knew of the whole affair had simply removed it and its contents, leaving an ordinary everyday briefcase.

Who?

Someone with easy access to the office and to the briefcase. Well, that could have been anyone who worked in the factory. But it had to be a narrower field than that.

It was someone who had pushed the idea of a personal visit to New Zealand. More, that person had engineered the visit to that particular furniture retailer, because that was the only place the switch of briefcases could have taken place, as my hotel hadn't been pre-booked – I'd picked one at random in a convenient city area when I arrived.

With a tight, sick feeling in my stomach I realized it had to be one of only three people: Martin, Nigel, or Gordon.

I tried to remember exactly what part each had played. The letter from the Auckland retailer had been sent to Gordon, but Martin had written to the retailer to enquire if they would interested in having more details of Selbridge furniure. But he had written to several retailers – and Gordon had given the addresses. But then, where had

Gordon got those addresses from? Anyone could have given them to him. Almost anyone in the factory *could* have sown the seeds of the idea – and suddenly it occurred to me that it didn't have to be an employee. Rachael or Eleanor or Christine could have unobtrusively launched the idea, although I found it hard to imagine any of them, and almost impossible to think of Eleanor – the Eleanor of that time – involving herself in anything.

Of the employees, only Otto Klein could be thought to be so involved in the affairs of Selbridge Furniture that some sort of suggestion of expanding markets could be made to sound a natural thing. I could hardly picture Otto in the role of running international contraband, but it would be foolish to dismiss anyone too lightly as being beyond suspicion.

Nigel had been lukewarm about the whole thing. Or had seemed lukewarm. He had agreed readily enough to go. Would he have done that if he'd been personally carrying something illegal? Well, it had been perfectly safe for me, so no doubt whoever the guilty person was he could have taken – or brought – the stuff personally. In the event, of course, Nigel hadn't gone because he'd developed flu.

And who had changed the briefcases over at the other end? The large unsmiling general manager? Not necessarily.

Again, anyone in the establishment could have switched the briefcases. I'd left Nigel's briefcase in the manager's office when he took me out for a cup of coffee, and then I'd left it with him over night so that he could discuss the possible deal with his sales manager, but that idea might not have been his own, either.

Obviously the thing had been very carefully planned. The contact at the Auckland end must have had an identical briefcase ready, initials and all. That could have been done by the person at the Australian end having sent an identical case in advance, so that not only the exact case but one with the exact lettering style for Nigel's initials could be ready.

The set-up had been careful, detailed, expertly planned. Therefore the stakes had been high. How much extra weight might I have carried without noticing it? Half a kilogram? Certainly that much. Probably a kilogram. The case had been quite weighty, and certainly jam-packed.

I sat for a long time just looking at the case and thinking, trying to recall if I had felt at any time that it weighed more than it had before. Or weighed less. Had I carried payment one way and goods the other? Probably not.

Because then the same case, with the false bottom or whatever it may have had, would have sufficed for both crossings of the Tasman. I had carried goods. I had been delivery-boy, not banker. Some other arrangements had been made for that. No doubt that would have been easy enough.

The most probable commodity for me to have carried would be drugs – probably heroin. Only drugs or precious stones would be really valuable in the quantity I could have carried without noticing anything unusual, and drugs seemed the much more likely.

I rubbed my hand over my face, carefully packed everything back into the briefcase, put the case back where it had been, switched off the lights and went out to my car. It was almost three in the morning, and there was a subtle change in the weather. Overhead the stars were still flung across the black in their glittering brilliance, but in the north-east they had vanished in a solid darkness that hung above the town's lights, and a wind was stirring fitfully, scattering the last flowers off the poinciana tree so that they looked like tumbling flame-coloured butterflies in the headlights as I drove out of the yard.

I ached with weariness and I was going home to bed. I had no idea what I should do about the briefcase. One part of my brain told me I should tell the police, of course. Another part told me to stop and wonder how much notice they would take of me. What evidence did I have to back up my story? Not a shred.

And if they began asking questions, whoever was behind the whole thing would know I was the person behind the police interest. Whoever was playing for big stakes would not be pleased with me.

Keith Barnes had telephoned Nigel with an urgent request to see him in private – which suggested Keith had some important information about something – or someone – which he wanted to talk about to Nigel. And Keith had been murdered before he could talk.

Had he stumbled across the same secret I had stumbled across? He had always been a man filled with curiosity about everything that went on – a prying kind of man. It was quite possible he had found something much more definite than I had found. But if that was the reason he had been killed, then I would be well advised to tread very carefully, because certainly I was on dangerous ground.

It was growing daylight before I fell asleep, and I slept till mid-morning. When I woke I had no better idea what I should do.

I drove around to Rhelma's place after lunch, as arranged, and we went in my car up the range to Martin's place to begin one of our regular week-end rides. The air was mercifully much cooler, with an overcast sky, though it was still heavy with humidity and the promise of rain, and a strong wind gusted fitfully.

'It looks as if the cyclone's certainly heading this way,' Rhelma commented. 'I think we'd better settle for a short ride this afternoon – it's sure to start raining pretty soon.'

'Cyclone?' I paused in the act of tossing a saddle across Mindy's back. 'What cyclone?'

'Haven't you heard any news lately?' Rhelma looked amused. 'The television news was full of cyclone warnings last night and the radio's been giving out hourly reports today.'

I shook my head. 'I didn't watch the TV news last night and I haven't had the radio on this morning. I overslept, as a matter of fact.'

She glanced at me. 'You don't look as if you overslept. You look more as if you haven't slept for a week. Anyway, there's a small but intense cyclone bearing down from the north-east, and by all reports it's expected to cross the coast just north of here, probably within twenty-four hours, so we could be in for some rough weather.'

'I've never been in a cyclone,' I said, 'so it'll be a new experience.' Then a flicker of alarm danced along my nerves. 'Martin's gone surf-board riding!' I said sharply. 'There'll be big seas building up.'

Rhelma smiled. 'He'll be perfectly all right. He's pretty expert on a surf-board, and board-riders love big seas. Anyway, it won't be really bad yet.'

She seemed more relaxed, more animated, than at any time since Keith's death. Perhaps at last she was beginning to come to terms with it, and with the fact that the murderer might never be caught.

.It was quite pleasant out riding, though I could see by the thickening clouds off to the east, along the coast, that rain was certainly building up and Rhelma's suggestion that we cut our ride short was justified. Rhelma seemed to be enjoying herself. She was a keenly observant person, quite knowledgeable about the native trees along the roadside and in the farms we passed, and I always enjoyed her company.

It was she who noticed the baby bird. A large spreading tree which by now I had learned was a Moreton Bay fig grew close beside the road. I heard the sharp calls of birds in the tree over our heads as we rode by, but in my city-bred ignorance I didn't recognize them as distress calls, but Rhelma pulled up her horse, looking upward.

'Now what's upsetting you?' she asked.

'Who?' I asked, a bit startled.

'The fig-birds. See, there? That's the male, that chap with the olive-green back and the red ring around his eye, and there's the female in the buff with brown flecks. Oh-oh. There's the trouble.' She pointed to the foot of the tree where an obviously young bird, like the female in colouring but clearly not yet able to fly, squatted awkwardly on the ground, hunched and miserable and an easy prey to any kind of predator from snake or hawk to passing cat or fox.

'He's fallen out of the nest,' I said, stating the obvious. 'Can you see the nest?'

We spotted it after a few minutes of craning our necks – a rather flimsy-looking structure near the end of a long branch.

'Poor little chap,' I said, dismounting. 'I think I can climb up there and put him back. I used to be a dab-hand at tree-climbing twenty years ago – there wasn't a boy in our suburb could climb higher or faster than I could.'

'Don't be daft!' Rhelma protested. 'You'll break your neck if you fall from that branch!'

'I won't fall,' I said cheerfully. 'Just let me get up on to the first branches and then hand me the bird up. I'll bet I can get him all the way back to the nest.'

'Holding him in one hand and hanging on with the other? You're crazy.'

'No more than usual. And I'll put him in my shirt-pocket so I can use both hands for climbing.'

I pulled my riding-boots off and headed up. Enough of my childhood expertise, which had almost given the neighbours heart-failure and prematurely aged my long-suffering parents, remained with me to let me get as far as the nest-branch reasonably easily. But once arrived there at that branch the only way to the clustered foliage at the end, where the nest was, was to crawl along the otherwise bare and ever-narrowing limb.

At age eight I should probably have enjoyed it immensely, but at age twenty-five I found it far from entertaining. But I was too egotistical to admit it, and somehow I got to the end of that wavering branch, sat astride it, gripping with my left hand and my thighs while I carefully took the little feathery bundle from my pocket and returned it to its nest beside a brother or sister while the parent birds made alarmed noises around me.

Then, sweating more with sheer fright than either heat or exertion, I edged back to the trunk and the descent from branch to branch until I could drop thankfully back to earth.

Rhelma watched me as I put my riding-boots back on. 'And you're the same person who's too nervous to go out deep-sea fishing? I know which I'd rather do!'

I looked up at her and grinned sheepishly. 'If you want the truth, my knees are shaking so much my legs feel like jelly and I'm going to be hard-pressed to climb back into the saddle.'

She laughed. 'That makes me feel better. I hope that poor little bird appreciates what you did for him.'

We rode on. I hadn't really realized I was too absent-mindedly lacking conversation until Rhelma said quietly: 'What's wrong, Trisha?'

I looked at her quickly, taken aback. 'Sorry,' I said. 'I guess – well, the funeral yesterday, and all that – '

I stopped.

'No,' I said eventually. 'It's not that. Or not only that. Do you remember, the morning I was going to New Zealand, I tripped and almost fell on one of those steel stakes that are used as supports for young trees in the factory yard?'

'Yes,' Rhelma nodded. 'I do remember thinking at the time you almost cut your hand on the post.'

'I scratched the bottom of the briefcase instead. Last night, because I was a bit up-tight after the funeral and everything, I couldn't sleep, so I went to the factory to catch up on some business letters and general office work to try to take my mind off other things. I had to get some papers out of the briefcase, for the first time since the New Zealand trip. There wasn't any scratch. Someone in New Zealand switched briefcases. Not the contents. Everything was exactly as it should have been. But it another briefcase. You don't have to be a genius to reach the conclusion that I carried something across the Tasman for someone. The question is: what did I carry, and for whom? And what do I do about it?'

Rhelma said softly, 'Oh, my God.' Then, sharply, '*Have* you done anything about it?'

'No. What can I do? Go to the police? What proof do I
have that there ever was a little cut on the bottom of the
briefcase?'

'Who might have handled the briefcase before you went?'

There was an intensity about the question which made me
glance at her. She was white-faced, her eyes dark with some
emotion which might have been fear or anger, and her hand
on the reins was gripped as tightly as if she were clinging to
something for life itself.

Instantly I was wary. With a sharp shock I realized that I
was wading in unknown waters and at any moment I could
well be out of my depth in heaven knew what violent
currents. *Rhelma?* Nonsense. But –

I shrugged. 'Oh, anyone could have. I don't know. Maybe
I'm just imagining things. Maybe there really wasn't a
scratch on the case to begin with. I wasn't in a very bright
frame of mind that morning. I certainly haven't anything
concrete to go on, and I certainly can't go running to the
police, or anyone else, for that matter.'

Rhelma hesitated, and then said, 'No, I suppose not.'

But I had a feeling that was not what she had been about
to say.

'That wind's getting stronger,' I said. 'I'm sure it'll be
raining very soon, too. Let's turn back.'

Martin's place was still deserted. We unsaddled the
horses, groomed them and put the saddles and bridles in the
little tack-room in the stables. The first heavy rain was just
starting as we ran out to the car – a quick, sharp shower. By
the time I dropped Rhelma at her house fifteen minutes
later the rain was almost constant, though erratic – one
moment little more than wind-swept mist and the next
pelting down in swirling sheets.

I had dinner and went to bed early, utterly wearied by the
emotions of the last few days and my almost complete lack
of sleep the previous night, and I slid down into heavy sleep.
I didn't wake until after four-thirty with summer dawn
struggling to filter faint light through the great depth of

cloud which must have been towering over us. I wondered how on earth I'd been able to sleep. Unrelenting rain was being crashed against the walls and across the roof of the block of flats by a mad wind which made a curious sound I had never heard before – above and intermingled with the normal roar of wind: a strange moaning howl which people were to tell me later was typical of a cyclonic wind, though no one could tell me why it was so.

I switched on my bedside lamp, relieved to find that the power supply hadn't failed yet. The radio informed me as I made coffee that the cyclone was expected to cross the coast, coming in from the sea, a little to the north of us in four or five hours time. Residents were warned to take all possible precautions – to take any outdoor furniture indoors, secure any loose objects outdoors which could be blown in the wind, check that pets were securely housed and, as the wind strength increased, to slightly open one or two windows on the opposite side of the house to the one the wind was striking, to reduce the risk of a build-up of pressure from inside the house possibly bursting outward, with structural damage that would then allow the wind to wreak more havoc. People were urged to remain indoors unless it was absolutely essential to go out. There had already been reports of some damage, and further damage and local flooding was expected.

I turned the radio off, made toast and sat down to eat. I wasn't hungry enough for coffee and toast at five in the morning, but it seemed as good an excuse as any for delaying a decision over what I must do about the briefcase.

I think I had already reached that decision – had probably known what I must do right from the moment my fingers had slid over the unscarred vinyl surface. Certainly by the time I had finished my coffee I was no longer hesitating. I put on a raincoat over shirt and jeans and jammed a rainproof hat on my head. I would go to the police. They could make whatever they liked of my story, believe it or disbelieve it, investigate with alert interest or dismiss me as an imaginative crank. But I must tell them.

To fail to do so was nothing but cowardice. I ruefully reflected that cowardice seemed the prudent course of action, and certainly infinitely more attractive.

But before I went to the police I must check that briefcase once more – must be absolutely certain I had not made a mistake; must be absolutely certain there really was no scratch, no little cut in the vinyl. It was just faintly possible the scratch wasn't exactly where I thought it was and, in the shock of not finding it and the rush of ugly thoughts that had precipitated, I had missed it. I didn't really believe that was even a possibility, but I must know beyond all doubt before I went to the police.

The rain hissed across the street and lashed into my face like fine hail as I unlocked the car. As I drove I could feel the car rocked slightly by the wind-gusts which drove the rain almost horizontally, and in low-lying places the streets were inches deep in water where the storm-drains couldn't cope. The weather bureau was right: it was a good day to stay at home unless one had urgent business.

The factory was of course deserted. As it was Sunday it would be deserted all day, but at this early hour there wouldn't have been anyone about anyway. I parked my car close to the front door and got out my key before I left the car, but even so I was drenched from the knees down before I got the factory door open. A rush of rain swept in with me and I almost had to lean on the door to close it. Because of the heavy cloud it was still almost dark inside the factory and I stepped forward, running my hand along the wall for the light switch.

As I did so my foot struck something soft but heavy and I almost fell. I snapped the light on and stood staring at Rhelma Barnes as she lay face down on the floor at my feet, a thick dark-brown stain spread on the floor from under her.

Eleven

Somewhere in my stunned brain I remembered you weren't supposed to move a body, however slightly, until the police had seen it. And close behind that thought came the recollection of the feel of her body as my foot had struck it: limp, inert. But not cold or rigid.

'Rhelma!' I whispered, and knelt beside her, reaching for a wrist. She was cold, but not with the chill of lifelessness, and under my fingers a pulse still beat.

'Rhelma!' I cried. 'Hang on! Hang *on*!'

I didn't stop to think that my voice fell on unconscious ears. A thread of life still ran through her being, and I was filled with a terrible urgency lest it should snap. I lunged into the office, dialled the triple-zero emergency number and begged breathlessly for police and ambulance.

A disembodied voice asked on behalf of the ambulance what was the nature of the accident, and I heard myself say: 'It's not an accident. It's attempted murder.'

Until that moment I hadn't consciously thought about it, but I knew it was true. Even then it didn't occur to me to wonder how long ago the would-be killer had struck, and whether he might still be in the factory. I didn't begin to think of that until I had gone back to Rhelma, dragging off my raincoat to put over her because the only thing I could think of was that an injured person was in shock and should be kept warm.

I looked around me, trying to think, to grasp some inkling of what had happened here.

It was only then that I noticed there were other bloodstains on the floor, smears on the tiles back along the passage to the door of the office. I went slowly back to the office, carefully this time, so that I didn't step on any of the stained areas, though I could see in a few moments that the blood there was dry. It almost looked as if she had been dragged along the floor – but hours before, for the blood to have dried.

At the door of the office I stopped. A few moments before, when I had run to the phone, I hadn't had any eyes for anything around me. Now I saw with a clarity which would have been sickening if I hadn't been too filled with blazing anger against whoever had done this to her.

There was blood on the chair in front of the desk, and a little to one side was a dark pool of it, still sticky-looking and not dried because there was too much of it. There was the imprint of a shoe, plain on the soft beige carpet. Then the dragging smears into the passage.

And on the carpet, as if dropped there in uncaring nonchalance, lay a knife with a blade perhaps six inches long and a wooden handle which even I thought bitterly would have been carefully wiped clean of prints. It was a knife which usually lay around the office and was handy for a great many things like cutting tape on packages. Probably it had originally come out of one of the workshops, most likely the upholstery section, but it had been aound the office ever since I'd come here. There were always knives of various kinds around the workshops. The killer hadn't had to look far for his weapon. And having used it he had tossed it almost defiantly on the floor: 'There's your murder weapon. See what you can make of that.'

I went back to Rhelma, and as I knelt again beside her, talking to her – saying heaven alone knows what, for I have no recollection of it except that I kept saying any reassuring things which came into my head, useless as they were to anyone deeply unconscious – I heard the wail of sirens.

I'd completely forgotten the violent weather until I opened the door and the rain lashed into my face as two ambulance

the door and the rain lashed into my face as two ambulance
men ran in to crouch over Rhelma, swiftly but gently pulling
back the raincoat I had put over her.

'She's been stabbed,' I said, standing back to let them
have plenty of room to move.

'Stretcher – and alert the hospital,' one said, working with
experienced hands to cut away Rhelma's blouse whose dark
material had prevented me from immediately realizing the
wound was in her back. More sirens shrieked to a halt and
two uniformed policemen came in, ushered by another blast
of wind and rain.

One looked curiously at me and, with a word to the
second man, who was bending over Rhelma helping the
ambulance bearers get her carefully on to the stretcher, he
ran out into the rain.

I wanted to shout at the ambulance men: 'How bad is it?
Will she live?' But I held my tongue and they didn't even
look at me, so intent were they on what they had to do, and I
knew they couldn't really tell me, and I must not delay them
even for a minute. There was a fearful lot of blood on the
hall tiles and soaked into the office carpet. Quite apart from
whatever organic damage that knife-blade had done,
anyone who had lost that much blood needed help with
terrible urgency.

I went on standing in the hall as the ambulance screamed
off into the wind and rain, the police car leading the way
with its blue lights flashing and siren adding a double
warning to any other road-users that a life hung in the
balance. It told me, if I needed to be told, that the
ambulance men believed Rhelma was very close to death.

The remaining policeman looked at me again, more
closely this time. 'I think you'd better sit down, Miss Kent,'
he said almost gently.

'I can't go into the office,' I said numbly.

His eyes followed the trail of bloodmarks on the tiles.

'She must have been stabbed there,' I explained. 'And I

mustn't touch anything, must I? Though of course I had to use the phone, before.'

He smiled. 'There must be somewhere else you can sit down. You rather look as if you need to.'

I turned and went into the upholstery workshop and sat on a bench. The constable was right: I was shivering with cold which had nothing to do with the temperature, and my knees felt perilously weak.

'Are you all right?' he asked.

'Thank you.' I nodded, and he went back, looked into the office without entering, and then opened the front door. I heard the rain and wind blast in, and then there were voices and I guessed more police had arrived. I sat silently, everything that was going on around me somewhat lost in the silent clamour of questions that were chasing through my brain.

I don't know how much later it was that two men came into the upholstery shop in slacks and open-necked shirts which suggested they had both dressed hurriedly. I recognized one as Detective Sergeant Cunningham, who had been in charge of investigations the night Keith had been murdered.

He looked me over with those keen blue eyes for a moment before he spoke. 'Good morning Miss Kent. This is Detective Holland. Perhaps you would like to tell us why you came here this morning?'

I told them about the briefcase. Detective Holland, an athletic-looking young man with straw-coloured hair darkened by rain, wrote in a notebook with an air of unobtrusive efficiency. Sergeant Cunningham never took his eyes off me and said absolutely nothing until I finished. There was nothing in his face to give the least hint of whether he believed a word I was saying.

When I had finished he said, 'So there was some doubt in your mind as to whether there was anything odd about the briefcase?'

'I wanted to be quite certain there really was no scratch before I made a fuss.'

'And so you came out very early in such bad weather? Why not leave it till later?'

'It had plagued me long enough. I'd made up my mind what to do, and I thought I'd better do it before my courage failed me.'

'Why should it require any particular courage?'

I stared. 'Keith Barnes had phoned Nigel Selbridge to arrange a meeting in circumstances which suggested he had something very important to say. Keith was murdered before he could say it. I wondered if I had stumbled on the same thing he had discovered. From that point, it wasn't too hard to begin wondering if I might meet the same fate if it became known that *I* knew something which might stop whatever kind of trade was going on.'

'Trade.' He didn't exactly make it a question, and I didn't answer. He was perfectly capable of reaching all the conclusions I had reached – and doing it much more efficiently.

'Thank God I did come,' I said suddenly. 'Rhelma would have died, surely, before tomorrow – which is when she'd have been found in normal circumstances.'

His face was still expressionless. 'Yes. Exactly where was Mrs Barnes when you came in?'

'Just inside the door. In the dim light I didn't see her until I stumbled over her.'

'And what did you do then?'

'I switched on the light and knelt down to see if she was alive. Then I went into the office and called the ambulance and police. Then I went back and put my raincoat over her to try to give her a bit of warmth. Before I had time to think of anything else the ambulance came.'

'Have you any idea why Mrs Barnes would have come here? Or how she would get in?'

'Keith would have had a key. All the factory employees have keys. I suppose she still had it at home and used that. As to why she came, I told her yesterday about the briefcase. She seemed to be – almost too interested, as if it were something personally important to her; so I then tried to make light of it and say maybe it was all a mistake on my part. She let the subject drop, but I think she may have decided she wanted to look at the briefcase for herself. It's always been terribly bitter for her that Keith's killer hasn't been found. She may have felt, as I did, that there was a connection.'

The sergeant said, 'Who else have you told of your suspicions about the briefcase?'

'No one.'

'Why did you tell Mrs Barnes?'

I hesitated. 'I'm not sure. She saw I was concerned over something and asked what it was. I hadn't intended to tell anyone.'

'When you went into the office to telephone, what exactly did you see?'

'Blood on the chair by the desk, quite a lot of blood on the floor, and a knife on the floor. It's a knife we commonly use around the office. It was probably on the desk or one of the filing cabinets.'

'Did you see the briefcase?'

I shook my head. 'No.'

'Where is it normally kept?'

'The last time I saw it was when I put it back in the cupboard to the left of the door.'

'And that's where it's usually kept?'

'Well, not always. It's Nigel's, so I suppose he often takes it home with him. I know I've often enough seen it around the office, but not necessarily in that cupboard.'

'Other members of the staff or the company would have briefcases? Gordon Selbridge? Martin Weldon? Yourself?'

'Gordon and Martin have black attaché cases. I don't have any.'

He nodded, got up from where he had been sitting on the arm of a chair-frame and went out to the office. Detective Holland asked a few questions about the time I had left Rhelma at her house and what I had done later, and after a while Sergeant Cunningham came back, carrying the briefcase by means of a piece of wood slipped through the handle.

He laid it down on the bench beside me. 'Is this the one?' I nodded, and he said, 'Where was the scratch?'

'On the bottom – just about there, as I remember it,' I said, pointing.

'You're absolutely certain there was a scratch? It couldn't have been something temporarily stuck to the surface?'

'No. It was scratched.'

He looked at me, a long silent look, and the longer he remained silent the more I began to wonder whether I could have imagined the whole thing.

Then quite unexpectedly he said, 'Thank you, Miss Kent. You can go home now. Please drive carefully. The wind is geting stronger – should peak in an hour or so – and there are sure to be branches down off trees and perhaps power-lines down.'

He wasn't a detective any more, just a rather pleasant, quiet man concerned for my welfare. I said, 'Can you give me any idea how bad Rhelma is?'

'I've spoken to the hospital, but they can't tell me much yet. She was stabbed once from behind as she sat at the desk in the outer office, it appears. Then apparently her attacker stabbed her again from in front as she lay on the floor, but the knife missed her heart. It seems surgery may be needed to determine just what organic damage has been done, but the most urgent thing she needs is quite considerable amounts of blood. They weren't able to tell me whether she might live. If she does, then of course our job will be easy because she can tell us who attacked her.'

'Damn him,' I said with tight bitterness.

He looked at me. 'You and Mrs Barnes are good friends?'

I nodded. Then I said sharply, 'You say she can identify her attacker. But you said she was stabbed first from behind as she was sitting at the desk. She might never have seen him.'

'We rather think she did. I don't doubt she may never have guessed he would try to kill her – you wouldn't normally sit down with your back to someone you suspected was about to attack you. But there is no sign of forced entry, no indication that theft was a motive for the peson being in the building. Both Mr Gordon Selbridge and his brother have come in – at our request – and they say nothing is missing from the office or the safe.'

'Gordon and Nigel are here?'

'Yes. Mr Nigel Selbridge says he hasn't seen his briefcase since you took it to New Zealand because he hasn't had any occasion to use it.' He smiled faintly.'We didn't tell anyone the reason for our interest in it, I assure you.'

'What about Martin? Martin Weldon? Is he here?'

The sergeant raised an eyebrow slightly. 'No. Should he be?'

The question caught me off guard and I felt my face flush. 'Since he's the accountant I thought you might have wanted him here for some reason. If he was here I'd have liked to see him, that's all.'

'Is he a good friend of yours?'

'Yes,' I said.

Evidently I said it with some degree of feeling, because the sergeant smiled with a distinct twinkle in those intent blue eyes. 'I see. We will, of course, interview everyone connected with the factory, in time. But you must realize that this attack may have no connection with the factory at all. It could be something personal against Mr and Mrs Barnes. First Mr Barnes is killed, then an attempt is made to kill his wife.'

'You think she let her attacker in?'

'Or came with him. Or her. Either that, or the person had a key and let himself in. But Mrs Barnes almost certainly knew he was there. Unless she told him she was coming here, I fail to see how he would know, though it could have been a coincidence that he just happened to come in when she was here.'

A thought struck me. 'Where was the briefcase?'

'In the cupboard where you said it should be.' He paused, and then added gravely, 'I see no reason for not telling you that there is a mark on it which is almost certainly blood. That would suggest that it was close to Mrs Barnes when she was attacked, and that her attacker then put it away again. Your suspicions may not have any substance, Miss Kent, but I really would advise you not to tell anyone else about them – not anyone.'

We looked at each other for a moment. 'I wonder,' I said slowly, 'why he dragged her from the office out to the front door? If he intended to get her right away from the place, why did he change his mind? *I* couldn't have disturbed him. A lot of that blood was dried, though some was still sticky. She must have been attacked last night. Why bother to drag her out there and then leave her?'

His eyes steady on me, he said, 'If the attacker were a woman, she may have realized the body was too heavy for her to dispose of. But we think she was left where she fell, in the office. There is much more blood there than anywhere else, and I think she lay there for some time. Presumably she regained consciousness, and tried to crawl to the front door with some idea of summoning help.'

'But – why not use the phone on the desk right beside her?'

'We can only assume she was too weak or in too much pain to stand or even kneel in order to reach it. Or else – and no doubt more probably – she was half-delirious or only semi-conscious and not able to reason.'

I shuddered as I had a mental picture of the bright-haired, gentle-eyed girl I knew crawling blindly, numbed beyond thinking with pain and weakness, driven even so by some basic, primitive need to do something towards survival.

Another man came to the door and spoke to Sergeant Cunningham, who turned back to me. 'Miss Kent, may I see your left shoe?'

I slipped it off and the two men turned it over and looked at the sole, then the second man took it away and when he came back with it in a couple of minutes he looked disappointed.

'Thanks, Miss Kent,' he said briefly. 'There was a shoeprint on the carpet but it's almost certainly yours. You evidently made it when you used the telephone.'

I put my shoe back on and stood up, feeling cold. I was partly wet from the rain which was still being flung against the building under the howling gusts of wind, and my shoe was stained from where I had stepped in a not-yet-dry pool of a friend's blood. I was cold in body and soul.

'I'm going home,' I said.

Cunningham nodded. 'Of course. We'll want you to sign a statement later, but we'll be in touch about that. And please remember my warning.'

'Drive carefully and don't talk to strangers,' said Nigel from the doorway.

I jumped. He was too near the truth for comfort.

'Certainly the former, Mr Selbridge,' the sergeant said easily, and he and the detective went out of the upholstery shop.

Nigel stood looking at me. It was the first time I'd seen him since Gordon's toast to Julian, and Eleanor's accusation. Then I remembered that had occurred only about thirty-six hours ago. It didn't seem possible it was such a little time. There was something about his face which suggested he hadn't slept much, but I couldn't guess what he was thinking behind those hazel eyes and that unruffled smile.

His voice was concerned. 'Are you all right? You're shivering.'

I nodded. 'I'm cold. I got a bit wet coming here, but I think it's shock or something.'

'Hang on.' He went into his own office and came out with a sweater. 'Put this on.'

I obeyed. It was sizes too big, but I rolled the sleeves up and felt less bone-chilled.

'Nigel,' I said bleakly, 'who? *Who* did this? It was one of us – someone from the factory, I mean. The police say not necessarily, but it *has* to be. Otherwise why here? Why would she have come here if the whole thing wasn't tied up with the factory?'

He shook his head. 'I don't know, Trish. No more than I did over Keith. And unless Rhelma can tell them I have horrible feeling it's going to be the same brick wall. No one can be implicated and probably no one can be cleared. Certainly I can't. Once again, I was at home alone. Gordon was at home – except for when he drove over to see Mother after dinner. Christine took the children to see a special kids' film in town, picked them up afterwards, with no one to keep check on the times of her comings and goings. Eleanor was at home in her flat and has no car. But Eleanor is superbly fit from doing great stints of walking in past years, so the mere fact she hasn't a car means nothing – only makes it easier for her to have left the flat unnoticed. I don't know anything about Martin, but unless he's very fortunate he will have been home alone – no witnesses. A hard story to prove. God knows about the others who work here, but they were clear enough out of it when Keith was killed. I suppose you could even say Mother had no alibi for the time after Gordon left her.'

'My story's the same,' I said.

'You? You can hardly be a suspect.' He smiled. 'If you'd tried to kill Rhelma you'd hardly have come back here at such an early hour in such ungodly weather just to find the body. And when you found her alive you'd hardly have called an ambulance to try to save her – and let her talk. You're the only one of us safely in the clear. Why the devil *were* you here?'

I blinked. I hadn't had time to think of a story to cover that. 'I woke up and heard the rain and wind, and I had a sudden awful feeling I'd left the skylight louvres over the office open on Friday,' I said. 'I had visions of the place being full of water.'

He didn't seem to notice my hesitation, but just nodded. 'Well, I'd better go. A nice polite young constable is coming home with me to make a nice polite search of my flat for bloodstained clothes, even though they don't put it quite so crudely.'

He turned to go and then checked his step and looked back. 'And Trish – for God's sake remember the sergeant's warning, whatever it was.'

When he was gone the factory seemed suddenly empty, though I could hear voices in the offices and knew there was still plenty of activity going on around me. But I was no longer part of it. My part, whatever it had been, was played. I was no longer of interest nor of use. I'd been told to go home.

But the prospect of going home alone to my empty flat was intolerable. I had to talk. I had to talk to Martin. I needed him as I had never needed anyone in my life. With his arms around me, his face against my hair, the warmth and strength and *life* of his body against mine, I could lose these horrors that had crowded in on me.

I barely glanced at the police officer who opened the door for me to plunge, head down against the lashing rain, toward my car. The sergeant was right: the wind had strengthened until now it had a vicious force which was frightening – or would have been if I hadn't been so single-minded. I couldn't run against it, though I tried. Simply to walk into it was a physical battle. By the time I got the car door open I was wet again, but I scarcely noticed it. I drove as fast as I dared, but I was forced to pay some regard to Sergeant Cunningham's warning about driving with care. The windscreen wipers at times could barely cope with the rain, and there was a constant barrage of leaves and twigs and larger pieces of branches being wrenched off trees and shrubs and scattered across the road.

I didn't meet another car on the road up the range, and I began to think I was the only lunatic out. But I wasn't.

When I got close to Martin's house, which was some half a kilometre back from the edge of the escarpment and almost at the foot of a western-sloping hill, I could see a horseman, apparently coming back from the farm which was opposite

Martin's house, and across the creek. Even in the blur of the
rain there was no mistaking the way he sat a horse. It was
Martin, riding Mindy.

Why he had chosen to ride anywhere on such a morning I
couldn't imagine – probably, being Martin, for the sheer
exhilaration of going out into the howling storm. I pulled
the car off to the side of the road near his stables – where his
car was already parked. With some alarm I realized that the
bridge at the creek was a metre or more under rushing
brown water – quite impassable to a vehicle and even more
so, I should have thought, to a horse.

The erratic swirlings of the clouds, sweeping low across
the range, hid horse and rider for a moment, and then I saw
Martin was going to cross higher upstream, ignoring the
bridge. The creek was narrower there, and Mindy no doubt
could swim it safely. Martin saw me and waved. Somehow
everything about him conveyed the fact that he was enjoying
himself, and all my feelings of near-fear of the cyclone
seemed at once absurd. I laughed a myself and got out of the
car. I couldn't be much wetter and who cared?

The big mare didn't show the least sign of balking at the
water. She went in carefully but unhesitatingly and struck
out strongly, Martin sitting easily in the saddle. They made a
perfect picture of trust between man and horse. She went
across at an angle, swept downstream, naturally, by the force
of the current, but she would have made it comfortably
enough.

I saw the tree seconds before it struck them – a small tree
in full foliage which had been wrenched from somewhere on
the creek bank and swept down on the rush of the flood. I
screamed: 'Martin!'

But even if he had heard there was nothing he could do.
The next moment he and Mindy were entangled in the
dragging branches and swirled almost completely around to
face the bank they had just left. Then they were no longer
being pushed downstream. Suddenly they were held still,
and I remembered with a mixture of hope and horror that

there was a fence strung across the creek there, because normally it was a friendly, shallow little stream which cattle easily waded across. Evidently a couple of posts had been washed out by the flooded creek and, no longer anchored at ground-level, the fence was floating like a boom-gate across the stream.

Tree, horse, man – all had been stopped by the four snaring barbed wires of the fence. I didn't remember running down the few metres to the creek, but I was standing on the bank as Martin flung himself out of the saddle and struck out for the bank, grabbing my hand as I reached to help him, and then he was standing safe on solid ground and we were holding each other tightly.

Presently he held me away a little and looked at me. 'Trisha! What the devil are you doing here in this weather? You look like a drowned rat!'

I laughed shakily. 'That's a line that must really get you somewhere with all the girls. Oh, Martin, you gave me such a fright! As for why I'm here – I had to see you. Have the police been in touch?'

He looked puzzled. 'Police? I came in fairly late last night after being down at the Gold Coast, and I went straight to bed. All the phones up here are out this morning – water must have got into cables or junction-boxes or something. Why? What would the police want with me?'

'It's Rhelma. She's been stabbed.'

'Rhelma!' I felt his body jerk, and for the second time I wondered for a fleeting moment of jealousy if Rhelma Barnes meant something special to him, or had done at some time.

'I found her this morning. She – '

'*You* found her!' His eyes were dark with something like horror. 'Oh, my God. How? Where?'

'I went to the factory for something. She was on the floor unconscious.'

He was staring at me. 'She's not dead?'

'No, thank God. Or she wasn't. I don't know if she can live. The police said the hospital couldn't tell them. She – '

I stopped. Something penetrated through all my thoughts. It was a high-pitched frantic sound, but I knew it wasn't human. Instantly I was jolted back to the realities of the moment and I looked past Martin at the flooded, rushing muddy foam of the creek.

'Martin!' I cried. 'Mindy's trapped against the fence!'

The mare was threshing desperately, fighting to get free of the tangle of branches and wire. Every now and then she would go right under the water, which was still rising.

'We've got to get her out, quickly!' I said. 'Look – I think she's caught by one stirrup hooked through the wire. See – when she tries to pull away?'

He stood still, just looking at the mare.

'Come *on*!' I said.

His hand closed hard on my arm. 'We can't do anything,' he said, and his voice was flat. 'That farm dam upstream is giving way. The water will rise very quickly if that happens.'

'Then we've got to hurry.' I started forward, but he held me.

'Don't be a fool!' he snapped. 'We'll all drown if we try to get her out. She's in a frenzy. Like as not she'd pull us under with her even if the dam didn't give way first.'

'We can't just leave her!'

'We have to.'

I swung around on him. 'That day at the falls – she saved your life!'

'Do you think I've forgotten? But that's no reason to lose it now – just throw it away. I've just been in that water. We'd have no chance of doing anything.' He pulled me against him again so that I couldn't see the doomed horse. 'My darling Trisha, you want to save the world. Who else would have risked getting killed yesterday to put that baby fig-bird in its nest? I wouldn't want you to be any other way. But there are times when you have to be sensible and realize there's nothing to be done. Come, let's go. It's best you don't see it happen. It'll be quick when the wall of the dam gives way.'

'We can't!' I was sobbing now. 'We can't just *leave* her!'

'We have to. Get in your car – *now* – and follow me back to Eleanor's place. I imagine that's where we should be. That's where the police will come, so we may as well all be there.'

He gripped my hand and led me back to the car and helped me in. 'The horse is finished, Trisha. She had a good life and it's finished. Forget it. It's only an animal.'

He ran through the rain to his car and drove off.

I sat stunned. Somewhere inside me was an agony of shock so cruel I felt I didn't know how I would get through the next ten minutes of my life, let alone any more that may stretch ahead of me.

All I could think of in the first few blinding moments was Martin's voice saying: 'It's only an animal.'

And almost incongruously, from far back, I heard my former Melbourne employer saying: 'It's only the cleaning woman.'

What Martin had said before hadn't registered until he dismissed Mindy, but the instant he had said that, I knew.

Martin knew about the baby fig-bird. The only way he could have known about that was if he had been talking to Rhelma. And if he had been talking to Rhelma, it had been yesterday evening – when, according to him, he had come home late from the Gold Coast and gone straight to bed.

Twelve

I sat staring through the rain at the road he had just driven along. The pain inside me was as real as if I had suffered a physical injury instead of only an emotional one, but although the rain blurred my vision nothing was mercifully blurring my thoughts.

Martin – Martin whom I had loved and ten minutes ago wanted with every fragment of my being – had viciously, brutally, tried to kill an unsuspecting young woman who had tustingly talked to him about our afternoon ride. What else had she told him? Beyond reasonable doubt she had gone to the factory to check out something connected with the briefcase, her suspicions an echo of mine. Almost certainly she had asked Martin to go to the factory also. Why Martin? The answer, I reflected bitterly, was probably that she had turned to him for the same reason I had turned to him: because she trusted him.

Perhaps if the tree hadn't fallen I might not have been jolted away from that line of thought until it was too late. A big gum tree growing beside the road, twisted and rocked by the swirling wind but with too massive a trunk to bend before it, tore out of the rain-sodden ground by the roots and crashed right across the road, making it quite impassable to any vehicle.

I looked wildly around me as I leapt out of the car. My hurt, my feelings, could wait. Rhelma was in deadly danger. Fool! Why hadn't I seen that at once? Martin had told me to follow him to Eleanor's house. But he wouldn't be going there. He would go to the hospital. What he had to do, if she was still alive, was dangerous and high with the risk of discovery; but he must do it, because if she lived she would identify her attacker.

I heard the frantic whinny again and whirled around. In my own shattered anguish I had forgotten the doomed mare.

'Mindy!' I shouted, and began to run back to the creek.

Suddenly I no longer cared if I died in the attempt: I had to try to free her. There was nothing else useful in the world I could do at this moment when so much was needed so urgently. I couldn't get anywhere in time to warn the police or the hospital of what Martin had gone to do. My car was trapped between the fallen tree and the flooded creek. All the phones in this area were out. It seemed to me the only thing of any consequence left that I might do with my life was to try to save that trapped mare. And if I failed and we both drowned, at least I hadn't betrayed her as I had been betrayed.

'I'm coming, Mindy! I'm coming!' I kept calling uselessly. I went into the water a little way above her so that the rush of the current swept me up against her in the tangle of the branches of the small tree which had been her undoing. The twigs slapped and scratched at my face and hands and my legs bumped and scraped bruisingly against the submerged branches as I struggled through them, the water surging sometimes over my head.

Then I had hold of the saddle. 'It's all right, girl, it's all right,' I was gasping. 'I'm here. It's all – '

An eddy of water went over my head and left me coughing and gasping. Mindy incredibly was threshing about much less, but whether from hope or exhaustion I couldn't know.

If my theory was right and she was caught because one stirrup was entangled in the wire – and in the wild, surging confusion of water and flicking branches I had no way of telling whether it was so or not – she would be free if I could get the saddle off. When the branch had struck her and spun her around, it meant that the girth-buckle was on the upstream side – my side – and the force of the water was keeping me pressed against her. But to reach the buckle I would have to duck my head under the water and hope I didn't get trapped there.

In a more sane state of mind I would never have atempted it.

Under that water I could see nothing, so I shut my eyes to try to protect them from sharp twigs and broken branches of the submerged little tree. I pulled myself down into the water, holding the flap of the saddle with one hand and working the other down the girth till I felt the buckle. Then I grabbed the sodden leather strap with both hands and tried to undo it.

It wouldn't budge.

I came up for air and Mindy lunged and almost knocked my grip of her loose. 'Hold still, Mindy!' I shouted.

Again I went down, and again I failed. And again. I was sobbing with rage and anguish. Martin had left this lovely animal to die. If I couldn't stop him from killing Rhelma Barnes, perhaps in my frantic brain saving Mindy had become some small way to thwart him, even apart from the fact that I wanted to save her for herself.

I clawed at the strap, and this time I managed to drag the loose end through the first bar of the buckle.

I surfaced with a surge of elation. 'Hang on, Mindy, we might make it now!' Down again, and I heaved with all my waning strength, and suddenly the strap slipped off the tongue of the buckle and as I came up I pushed against the saddle and it lifted clean off Mindy's back.

I grabbed the trailing reins and, keeping hold of her neck, I urged her to turn, letting me stay up-stream of her. Now I had to pray that her legs were free, and it had been nothing more than the snagged saddle that was keeping her prisoner.

She came around and I ducked under her neck as she flung herself in a series of frantic lunges for the bank. My arms almost pulled from the shoulder-sockets, I managed to hang on to her bridle, and she dragged us both up on to the safety of the grassy bank. I let go and lay face down, choking and coughing and vomiting water.

I don't know how long I lay there, but it was probably no more than two or three minutes before I rolled over and scrambled to my feet. Mindy stood a couple of metres away. trembling but watching me with those intelligent dark eyes. I went to her and she put her velvety muzzle against my chest and I fondled her ears for a moment, talking nonsensical endearments to her. I was shaking quite as violently as she was, but as I stood with my arms about her neck, feeling some life come back into me, I began to realize that provided she wasn't too badly injured, I had a form of transport which wasn't deterred by a tree fallen across a road.

There was a farmhouse on the edge of the range no more than half a kilometre away – less if I cut across the paddocks, and Rhelma and I had often enough ridden that way, so I knew exactly where all the gates were. If the phone at the farm was out, at least they had vehicles – a car and a utility truck as I remembered it. There might still be a chance I could stop Martin, because even once he had arrived at the hospital he would have to wait his opportunity.

I ran quick, exploratory hands over Mindy. She had multiple cuts and welts of bruising, and normally I wouldn't have dreamed of riding any horse in such a condition. No decent person would. But she didn't seem to have any major injuries, and when I led her a little she didn't limp. I'd never ridden bareback in my life, but at that moment I scarcely stopped to think about that – except for the fact that without a saddle Mindy was too tall for me to mount. I led her to the fallen tree, scrambled up on the trunk at its thickest part and so onto Mindy's patient back.

She responded as readily as if she had just come out of a warm dry stable instead of a battering, suffocating torrent of water which had come within an ace of killing us both.

Perhaps it was a kind of shared exhilaration that we were alive and *doing* something, but there was, I am certain, a special bond between us as we raced across the paddocks, Mindy's hoofs cutting the sodden turf as I clung to her mane, feeling the bunch and stretch of her muscles with every stride.

I think we had gone perhaps several hundred metres before I realized there was no rain. As abruptly as if someone had tripped a switch, it had stopped. Perhaps it had stopped while we were struggling in the water, and I had been too preoccupied even to notice. I flung a quick glance skyward. The clouds were breaking up and the wind had fallen to almost nothing. Something like hope flickered inside me, down underneath the torment. The passing of the cyclone seemed to have some kind of significance.

As I reached down to open the last gate before the farmhouse the sun came out, bright and hot, as if it wanted to warm my aching spirit as much as my body, chilled under my soaked clothes. Two dogs bounded out, barking, as I pulled up at the garden gate, slid from Mindy's back and ran up to the front door.

There was no answer to my knocking. I called. I shouted. I ran across to the farm sheds, calling as I ran: 'Hello! Anyone there? Help me! Please!' A black and white cat came cautiously out of the barn, more wary of the weather than me.

There was no human there.

For a little while I couldn't believe it and kept calling. I ran back to the house and pounded on the door again. I went to the back door and tried the handle. It opened and I went in unhesitatingly and picked up the telephone. The line was dead. I ran out to the garage. Surely one of the vehicles would be there. If I could find the key I would take it.

The garage was empty. I began to cry, sobbing with rage against the injustice of it: how could everything work so totally together to stop me from helping Rhelma? Through a blur of tears and anger I looked down at the roof of Eleanor's house where it showed among the trees at the foot of the range – hundreds of feet below me but looking deceptively so close I might almost throw a stone on it. Yet by road it was at least ten kilometres away.

A great gust of wind howled through the trees, and another, and the sunlight was blotted up in clouds again, and almost at once the rain came sweeping back from the opposite direction from where it had blown from before, and the wind snatched at me as if it would pick me up and fling me bodily off the escarpment, down towards Eleanor's house.

I realized then what had happened: the eye of the cyclone had passed over us, with that curious pool of calm, bright weather before the passage of the centre of the great storm brought another quadrant of the whirlpool of wind and rain upon us.

And with the shock of the storm's return I was jolted out of my blind hysteria into purposeful thinking.

It seemed all the telephones in this area were out of order, and even if I went to another house and there were people and vehicles, I had no way of knowing if the road between here and town was trafficable. One tree had fallen; it was probable there were others, or a flooded creek had cut the road.

But just down below me was Eleanor's house, on an entirely different set of telephone lines. Between me and it there was no road, not even a track, but a few hundred metres along the edge of the range a ridge ran down at a steep but not impossible angle, and I had often seen cattle grazing on it. If cattle could get up and down, so could a horse.

I ran back to Mindy, who was standing where I had left her, tail turned to the gale, her brown coat still heavily streaked with blood from her cuts. 'Can you, Mindy?' I begged. I remembered just in time that this time I had no idea where there were gates – or whether there were any. A few moments search of one of the sheds produced a pair of wirecutters. I didn't dare stop then to think that the farmers might hate me bitterly for cutting fences and causing heaven alone knew what confusion in a mix-up of cattle.

I rode at a flat gallop down a stony lane to the top of the ridge I had in mind, the rain, wind-whipped, stinging my face like pellets of ice and the air full of flying bits of leaves and twigs. There was a gate and I dragged it open and flung it back and urged Mindy through. The mountainside was treacherously slippery and Mindy, wide-eyed with concentration rather than fear, went down in a series of sliding plunges, almost on her haunches, with her front legs propping stiffly on the steep slope, hooves alternately slipping and biting in the wet earth while I twisted my fingers into her mane, gripped with my knees and thighs and hung on like a desperate burr.

Once we dropped over the edge of the escarpment we were sheltered from the worst of the wind, but rain still streamed down my face and into my eyes. A couple of times a clump of bush loomed in front of us and once a fallen tree barred our way, but each time the big mare twisted broadside to the slope, skidding but never floundering, and edged carefully over the flank of the ridge and partly into the brush-filled gully on one side or the other. Then we would be around the obstacle, both of us with a few more scratches, and she would be plunging and sliding down again. Then the steep ridge was behind us and we were out into the howling wind again, on rough but more undulating ground, and almost at once we encountered a fence. I slid off Mindy and cut through the strands of barbed wire, the need for haste crowding almost everything else from my mind and giving my shaking hands strength I didn't know they had, while I cursed the dragging weight of my sodden clothes, and the rain that made the handles of the wirecutters slippery and half blinded me.

The country opened up into more friendly-looking pasture for a couple of hundred metres, and with hands and heels I urged Mindy to a gallop. I could have killed us both. In the long grass, neither of us saw the gully across our path, gouged out deeper and wider with the torrential rain.

Fortunately it was all so quick I had no time to do anything, because my instinct would have been to snatch back on the reins and try to pull Mindy to a halt – and she couldn't have stopped in time. I felt her jerk and bunch her muscles and I braced myself as she jumped. I had never jumped a horse over anything more than a six-inch log, but her skill made up for my incompetence. Somehow she cleared it and then in a moment we were at the house.

I ran up to the back door, calling: 'Christine! Christine!'

For the second time I had come to an empty house. Even above the wind and rain no one could have failed to hear me. Neither was there any response from Eleanor's flat when I pounded at the door. Only Tessa, the dog, whined hopefully from the laundry where evidently she had been shut for shelter from the weather, and now she was anxious for company. I couldn't take time to comfort her just now.

I didn't even stop to wonder where they had all gone. This time my brain functioned. When I had stayed here in the house when I first came to Queensland I had been shown where the spare key to the back door was kept hidden under a loose flagstone. My groping fingers found it now and I opened the door. Pehaps yet I would be in time to warn the hospital that the predator was out after his prey.

I ran into the lounge room and stopped.

Martin was sitting in one of the easy-chairs and he held a .38 calibre pistol pointed squarely at my face, and he was smiling.

'Do come in, Trisha, it's such foul weather out.'

I just stood there absolutely still, staring at him.

It was finished. Everything I had done. Everything Mindy and I had done together over this past – how long? Half an hour? It felt like half a lifetime. And it had all come to this.

'I must say I'm relieved to see you,' he was saying pleasantly. 'I really have had some most anxious moments wondering if I'd gambled wrongly, and you'd realized I'd given the show away by that stupid remark about the bird. But I waited outside the hospital and you didn't come, so I thought you'd come here.'

He raised an eyebrow. 'I did blow it, didn't I? You did pick up that little slip of the tongue, because you knew before you came in here. You got a terrible shock to see me, but it was no surprise at all that I have a gun trained on the love of my life. So why did you come *here*? Why not the hospital, or the police? Don't tell me you couldn't turn me in – not with your bloody conscience.'

The first hint of a crack in the courteous façade showed in a ring of momentary anger. Then I realized why he was puzzled. In the roar of wind and rain he couldn't have heard a car and he assumed I'd driven here.

'And how in hell did you get so filthy? What have you been doing?' The tone was not exactly sharp, but it was direct: he expected answers; he needed to know exactly what had happened.

I had no strength left, no will-power to defy him. For an absurd moment I was uncomfortably aware that I had tracked mud over Christine's good carpet and was even now dripping muddy water on it.

'A tree fell and blocked the road,' I said dully. 'I got Mindy out and rode here. There was no one home at the farm and the phones are out.'

His eyebrows rose. 'Well, well! Resourceful, aren't you? And a plucky little devil. If only you were more practical, we'd have made a good team. There's a fortune waiting to be made, you know.'

I just went on looking at him. I couldn't feel anything. Not fear, not anger, not revulsion. I concluded that was why I felt so empty, drained, lifeless. All that I had had was gone, and nothing had come to replace it. But there was something I wanted to know before he pulled that trigger.

'Why did you do it?' I asked.

'Do what?'

'Stab Rhelma. And kill Keith. I know you were smuggling – heroin, I suppose. But what did they know? Or guess?'

'Smuggling.' He smiled quite guilelessly. 'Somehow that

sounds a very quaint term. Old-fashioned. But then, you are
rather, aren't you? Yes, it was heroin. I have certain contacts.
On certain occasions when I go out deep-sea fishing I am not
only fishing. I meet ships at sea – or at least I pass near them.
Freighters in from the romantic East. If a crewman tosses a
package overboard, who will notice, even if it's equipped with
a marker buoy to keep it afloat? It doesn't happen often – that
would possibly attract attention. But the packages are quite
valuable, so there don't need to be many. I have varied the
method on occasion, such as when Nigel went to Hong Kong
and one or two other places. He brought some of the
merchandise back, although he didn't know it.

'Keith Barnes quite by chance found a package of the stuff
in one of the company's chairs which was on special order.
That's why I got a job with Selbridges, of course: upholstery
is an excellent hiding place, and who would ever dream a
respectable old firm like Selbridges would be using furniture
as cover for drug-running?

'Anyway, Barnes held his tongue and bided his time. Then
you went chattering about the damned first-aid box and me
taking it out on a fishing trip, and about the antiseptic
powder. And he knew there wasn't any such thing in the box,
damn him, and he twigged I brought the stuff ashore. I had
reckoned the first-aid box gave perfect cover for getting the
stuff into the factory. And if anyone opened the box the only
thing to notice would be a couple of plastic bags marked
"Antiseptic Powder". Who'd give it a second glance? It was
marked out of date, at that.'

Faint interest touched me. 'You asked me to go fishing with
you that day. What if I had?'

He laughed. 'I knew you wouldn't, and the fact I asked you
underlined the open innocence of my fishing trips. Barnes
phoned both Nigel and me to go to see him, that night. He
wasn't sure whether I was running solo or whether the
company was involved.'

He made a brief, contemptuous noise. 'The fool thought
he'd confront us and make us tell him all about it. With this.'

He moved the pistol fractionally. 'It made him too sure of himself, and for a moment he turned his back on me. The rest was easy. God knows whether he was going to hold us prisoner while he called the police, or whether he meant to kill us – or me. He had a fanatical hatred of anyone who dealt in drugs because it was someone woozy with marijuana who was driving the car that put him in a wheelchair. And he knew this was much bigger league than marijuana.'

I remembered Rhelma saying it was a driver 'under the influence of liquor or a drug' as the official term put it, and I had always assumed the driver had been drunk. Now I understood some of the things Keith had said.

Martin was saying: 'People are such fools. Rhelma guessed Keith had picked up some damning information on someone, of course, but she had no idea of what or who. Then you told her about the briefcase and she guessed what had been done, same as you did. But she was sure it was Nigel behind it all, and she didn't know whether you'd tried very seriously to find out if there was anything to be found out about that briefcase. So she phoned me as a friend, to come and help her try to find what was phoney about it – and of course, nothing is. Not that one. But she was too dangerous to let walk out of the factory and talk to police.'

'And now I am.'

'Oh, yes. Much too dangerous.'

'Your luck will run out. Three murders is stetching it thin, and you may not succeed in killing Rhelma.'

He shrugged. 'There will be nothing to link me with any of it.'

'Someone will have seen your car coming here. It's not such a busy road and traffic won't be particularly heavy on a morning like this. Or you might meet the others – Gordon and Christine and Eleanor – on the way back from wherever they are.'

'Oh, they've gone to the senior Mrs Selbridge's place. I phoned and told them I was a detective inspector and wished to see them all at their mother's home urgently.

Some of the roads are cut – it will take them quite a while to get there by a roundabout route, but they won't give up till they get there, because they'll be sure she's either murdered or arrested. And just as insurance I borrowed a van no one will miss and it will be safely returned to where I found it. I know the owner's away. So there's really nothing to point to me at all. I'm quite used to planning things.'

Complacency had always annoyed me. The monstrosity of his complacency now at last made anger begin to rise in me, replacing some of the emptiness, and with the anger came life.

'How many other murders have you planned?' I demanded.

'Oh, no others. I never set out to kill anybody. It's just been rather unfortunate that it became necessary.'

'What about the people who buy your damned heroin? It kills them in the end – or most of them – if they can't give it up.'

He shrugged. 'That's their problem. I don't force them to start using the stuff. If people are fools enough to get hooked it's nothing to do with me. I'm merely fulfilling a market requirement. As for the rest – you must understand that there is a great deal of money at stake. I certainly don't intend to let anyone stand in my way.'

'So money is more important than human life?'

He laughed. 'My dear girl, people are killed every day for much more trifling reasons than mine.'

'Even when it comes to a choice between taking what you've made and getting out of the business because someone was getting suspicious, or murdering, you choose to murder.'

He smiled. 'No one operates a drug-running business of any size entirely alone. And the other people involved are not at all enthusiastic about the idea of one member dropping out: he then is dangerous. Once in, you don't get out. So you don't go into this line of business if you're going to be squeamish about doing whatever has to be done.'

He made a small gesture which might almost have been of regret, or at least a strange kind of apology. 'I told you once that I had things to do, that I long ago vowed I wasn't going to live the kind of life my father lived. I vowed that I would make money. A lot of it. I have never particularly cared how.'

'And was making me fall in love with you all part of your grand plan?'

'No.' Just for a moment a shadow touched his face, and then he smiled again. 'But it proved a most delightful diversion.'

I had wondered vaguely why he had talked so much, told me of his activities. I understood the reason now. I had read once that a criminal was an egotist, and one of the hardest things for a successful criminal is that he can't tell anyone of his cleverness. I could see it was true of Martin. He could talk to me in safety because I was not going to leave this house alive.

The small flame of anger in me flared up into a blaze of fury. I had been standing all this time with my hands behind my back gripping the edge of a small table for support. Now I recalled that on this table Christine always kept a bowl of flowers. I saw Martin draw his feet under him to get up from the easy-chair where he was sitting, and I felt that if the muzzle of that pistol was ever going to waver for a moment from my face it would be in the next few seconds as he stood up.

My hand eased back until I felt crystal, and my fingers curled around the vase. As Martin began to stand up the pistol moved a fraction and I jumped sideways and, bringing my arm around in a sweep, flung the vase – water, hibiscus blooms and all – at his midriff.

The gun went off with a shattering crack which mingled with Martin's spat: 'Bitch!' But I felt no tearing impact of a bullet as I whirled and dodged back through the doorway I had entered from, between dining-room and lounge.

There was another shot and the sound of splintering wood as I ran blindly for the kitchen. I don't think I had any hope of survival. I was acting purely from a deep, primeval urge to fight for life, however hopeless that fight may be. My instinct was to get out into the open, but it was sheer unreasoning instinct. God knows, I had no intelligent thought at all.

I heard another splintering crash, but no shot. I had actually reached the kitchen door before I realized that that sound had been followed by a dull thud, and then there were no pursuing footsteps and no further shooting.

I stopped with my hand on the knob of the back door, and turned.

Martin lay crumpled on the dining-room floor, just inside the doorway. A man stood over him with part of one of Christine's dining-suite chairs in his hands. The rest of the broken chair lay beside Martin.

'I really must,' Nigel said, 'look into the design of these chairs. They're quite too flimsy. I do hope they're not Selbridges'.'

'Nigel,' I whispered. My legs felt as if they couldn't possibly support me and I leaned against the wall, shivering from head to foot.

The room was dim from the mass of the cyclone's cloud blocking out the sun, and in my blind flight I had rushed past him without seeing him. Obviously the same thing had happened to Martin.

Nigel picked up the revolver and kicked away the broken pieces of chair, and then looked at me and came quickly across the room to me, pulled up a chair and sat me gently in it. I gripped the edges of the chair for a moment while the room seemed slowly to cartwheel. Then it was steady again and Nigel was pushing a brandy into my hand and telling me to drink. The fire of the spirit spread slowly through my numbed body as I sipped, but I couldn't take my eyes off that sprawled figure on the floor.

'Is he dead?' I asked as soon as I∙had enough strength to raise my voice above the howling of the wind.

'Unfortunately no. But I rather think he won't feel very well for an hour or so. However, in case I underestimated him, as soon as you feel you can, would you phone the police? I'll just keep this handy to discourage any further violence on his part.' He held up the gun. 'Or would you rather keep guard over him while I do the phoning?'

I shook my head. 'Don't give that to me,' I said slowly. 'I might kill him.'

'Probably an excellent service to society,' Nigel said amiably, 'but unfortunately against the law.'

Then in a quite different voice he said, 'Are you hurt, Trish?'

I shook my head. 'I'll go and phone the police. I just want them to come and take him away.'

It was terribly true. I didn't want him in the same room or in the same house. I wanted him out – out of my life, though I knew he would not be out of my mind for a long time.

When I came back from the phone in the lounge-room Martin still hadn't moved.

'The police are coming,' I said flatly.

Nigel nodded, not taking his eyes off Martin. 'He killed Keith, of course, and tried to kill Rhelma? That's what all this was about?'

'Yes.'

'Why?'

'He was running a heroin racket, using Selbridge furniture as a means of distribution. Keith found a packet hidden in a chair that was on special order. Then – ' I shook my head. 'It's all complicated. You'll hear it all when the police come.'

'Martin. Martin Weldon.' His voice was low, so that I could hardly hear it above the wind. 'Dear Heaven. I thought it was Gordon.'

I jerked my head around to stare at him. 'You *knew*?'

'The time I went to Hong Kong and Thailand, I was nearly certain my luggage had been tampered with, but I couldn't *find* anything. But I did periodic searches of the furniture, because I wondered. And I found a packet, too. Maybe the same one Keith found. I thought it was just one isolated instance, and Gordon had somehow arranged it to raise money because he was broke and so was the company. So I did nothing. But it rattled me to my boots. That was why I wanted the company sold.'

'I see.' I thought a minute. 'Nigel, when you came here today, how did you know I was in danger? Why didn't you just knock, or walk in?'

'I saw Mindy in the yard, all cut about and in a lather, and there was a strange van outside, and I guessed something was wrong, so I just did a little snooping around the windows.'

'Mindy!' I cried, leaping up. 'I'd forgotten her. I must see to her – '

Nigel caught my wrist. 'Sit down. She's all right, I promise – just cut about. We'll get a vet out to look at her as soon as the police have finished here. It was just good luck I was in the right spot when you made a run for it. I was going to try to create a diversion and hope I could jump him before he could use the gun, but you made it easy.'

Martin stirred, moaned and sat up unsteadily. He made to get to his feet, and Nigel said, 'I wouldn't, if I were you.'

Martin turned his head and saw us both, and his eyes went to the gun. For a moment he was perfectly still, and then he put both hands to his head and slumped back.

'Oh, my God,' he said bitterly. 'The knight in shining bloody armour.' He gave a short hard laugh and his face was full of pure hatred. 'The local embezzler made good. The family will have to love you now, won't they?'

Nigel said nothing, and the wail of a police siren came above the wind.

It was a very long time and many questions and answers later, that Nigel and I sat in Christine's kitchen. I had showered and borrowed some of Christine's clothes and made coffee and sandwiches. It seemed a long time since I had eaten, but food was tasteless and hard to swallow.

The police had told us that Rhelma's condition had improved slightly and although she was still unconscious the

doctors were optimistic. A phone call told us Gordon and
Christine and Eleanor were at Rachael's house but would
be back as soon as that road was clear – perhaps in an hour.
The children were with friends. A vet had come and checked
Mindy's wounds and stitched several of the worst cuts. We
had let Tessa out of the laundry and, comforted by human
company, she lay dozing at Nigel's feet.

Now everything seemed a curious void, a flat and empty
aftermath. As the warmth of the coffee began to filter
through my veins I realized I ached all over and the muscles
of my thighs were painfully stiff from gripping Mindy's bare
back on my hectic ride, and my hands and legs were still
unsteady.

We ate our sandwiches in silence until something
penetrated my dulled senses and I said: 'Nigel, the rain's
stopped! And the wind has dropped a lot.'

He nodded. 'The cyclone's passed by. Often, after the
centre passes, it's all gone quite soon.'

A thought had been nagging just below the level of my
awareness, and now as it surfaced I put my cup down and
looked at Nigel.

'I'd be dead if you hadn't come when you did. Why did
you come here today? I mean, in this awful weather – why?'

He smiled wryly. 'Driven by some strange premonition?
I'd like to think so. No. It was something much more
concrete, and much less noble.'

He looked at me for a moment. 'I had a question that had
to be answered. I phoned, and no one answered, so I knew
the house was empty, and that was what I wanted because I
couldn't get my answer while there was anyone here.'

He hesitated. 'I still have my question. I guess the time
has come to get my answer, before the others get back.
Come. You may as well know it, too.'

He got up and I followed. 'Where are we going?'

'To Eleanor's flat.' He produced a keyring, selected a key
and we went in. 'Gordon and I have always had keys to the
flat,' he explained. 'To be able to get in if there should ever

be an emergency. It was Eleanor's idea,' he added.

I had a moment of sharp awareness of the fact that Eleanor West must have lived in a constant, half-submerged nightmare – a subconscious terror of once again being trapped in a locked room with no one able to open the door.

Nigel tossed his keys on to the table and went across to the door of her bedroom, which was open. He pulled the door closed and then stood for quite some seconds, just silent and with his head bent. Then he unbuttoned his shirt-pocket and took out a different key – an old-fashioned, much heavier key – and put it in the lock and turned it. I heard the tumbler of the lock click. Then he put his hand on the door-knob and tried to turn it, but the lock had gone home. Then he twisted the key again and opened the door.

He turned to look at me, his face beaded with perspiration, and finally I understood.

'That key! That's what you picked up beside Julian's body.'

He nodded slowly. 'It was just instinctive. I didn't want Eleanor to know about that key – even though I hadn't had time to think of what it was I didn't want her to know.'

I rubbed my face, hoping to clear my fogged brain. 'Then that's the key that was missing, the night of the fire.'

'Yes.' His face was grim. 'Julian West hadn't had the cellar filled in, and I made enquiries and the builders who did the renovations said they had never had any instructions to do so. On the contrary, I suspect he quietly worked to keep it readily useable. He wasn't trying to rescue his wife that night when the beam fell on him. He wasn't trying to get into the room. He was leaving it.'

We looked at each other for a long minute.

'Oh, God,' I said. 'Leaving it locked and burning. And two days ago I drank a toast in honour of his memory.'

Nigel smiled wryly. 'You needn't feel badly about that,' he said quietly. 'He saved your life.'

'Saved *my* life?'

'If it hadn't been for him, I wouldn't have come here today.'

'No,' I said soberly after a long moment. Then: 'What are you going to do?'

'Nothing.' He buttoned the key back into his shirt pocket and picked up his other keys from the table. Then he looked at me levelly. 'And neither are you.'

'But – '

'Trish, you've seen Eleanor. You know what she was like, before. You've seen what she's been like since Julian was found. She's my sister as she used to be. I can't take that from her.'

'The family will go on thinking you took the company money!'

'Does it matter? Anyway, Martin had a point: for putting a stop to his murderous activities everyone will have to think kindly of me and forgive my boyish trespasses.'

I was silent for a little while. 'What will you do?'

'Do?' He raised an eyebrow. 'Go off and find out what I'd be like at my chosen profession. Go and try to make it as an architect. That's what I trained for, remember?'

'Do you have to leave Selbridges?'

'Oh, yes, I think so. I always meant to, once the company could manage without me. And now I think it can.'

'But who will design?'

'You can. I told you once you've a flair for it. I've got quite a lot of designs drawn up, and you can study construction techniques before those designs run out. That new fellow we put on in place of Keith is good. Work with him.'

'Where will you go?'

'Hobart, I think. I went there once and liked it. I'll hang out my shingle and try my luck.' He touched his shirt-pocket. 'And drop this in the Derwent. Where it's deep.'

'Will you come back?'

'Oh, yes. I'll have to come back for the trial, I guess. But – oh, yes, I'm not going into exile. I'll come back.'

There was the sound of a car and he glanced down the road. 'There are the others coming. Christine and Eleanor will look after you – and you'll need looking after for a few days, I think. I'll go. I don't really want to have to face them right now. I'll say my goodbyes later.'

He stood looking down at me, hazel eyes steady. Then he thrust his hands deep into his trouser-pockets.

'Damn it, Trish, why did you have to fall in love with the wrong man?'

He turned on his heel without another word and strode out to his car and drove away, leaving me standing numbly. Slowly I became aware of a curious scent, and realized it was the smell of leaves torn and crushed by the wind, lying thickly on the ground, plastering the roof and walls of the house like ragged green confetti. It was the smell of a storm-battered world.

Mindy made a soft little whickering noise and I turned and saw her watching me, head over the garden fence, and I went to her and put my arms around her neck.

As the car came up the drive and stopped and Eleanor got out and came quickly, concernedly, towards me, I looked at the spot where Julian West had died, and saved my life. Maybe one day when the hurting had gone out of me, I could drink a toast to him again.

If you have enjoyed this book and would like to receive details of other Walker mystery titles, please write to:

Mystery Editor
Walker and Company
720 Fifth Avenue
New York, NY 10019